"Jesus," Campbell muttered as he furiously tried to reload his rifle. When he did, he settled on one knee to steady himself, remembering the advice Sharp had given him a few days earlier: "Ye ary have to face a buffler head on, hoss, shoot for the chest. Ye hit that critter in the head and all you'll do is get yourself stomped into the ground. A buffler's head is the hardest kind of thing, this chil's sayin' to ye."

Heart in his throat, Campbell forced himself to wait as long as possible, wanting to get off as good a shot as he could, considering he was only going to get one. At last he fired, but the buffalo kept coming. The bison finally went down a few feet later, sliding along on his chin whiskers.

"Dear mother of Christ," Campbell breathed as he shoved to his feet and then jumped. The buffalo carcass slid under him, and he came down atop it, twisting an ankle a little and falling off to the side. He scrambled up, heart pounding, but saw that the buffalo was dead.

By the same author

Mountain Country series:

Southwest Thunder
Winter Thunder
Mountain Thunder

Available from HarperPaperbacks

BUCKSKINS
AND
BLOOD

JOHN LEGG

HarperPaperbacks
A Division of HarperCollinsPublishers

HarperPaperbacks   *A Division of* HarperCollins*Publishers*
                    10 East 53rd Street, New York, N.Y. 10022

Cover illustration by Tony Gabriele

First printing: August 1994

Printed in the United States of America

HarperPaperbacks and colophon are trademarks of
HarperCollins*Publishers*

❖ 10 9 8 7 6 5 4 3 2 1

1

A small flock of kestrels fled, squawking, from a wolf's willow, whirling into the late afternoon sky, angry at being disturbed. The two men sitting by a fire in the small mountain meadow gave each other one quick glance and then faded into the brush and trees nearby.

"Sounds like two, three horses," one whispered to the other.

The tall, broad-shouldered one grunted an affirmative. "I'll jist take me a quick *paseo* and be certain," he said. Then he disappeared without a sound; there one second, gone the next. He returned just as silently. "Ain't but one, and he's a critter new to these places," Ethan Sharp said quietly.

"Sounds like it," Caleb Finch noted as he heard snapping twigs and other assorted noises.

They crouched behind an azalea bush, silent now, their rifles ready, listening to the solitary man struggling through the underbrush on the opposite side of the meadow from them.

Finch and Sharp had been in the mountains eight years now, yet neither was near thirty. It was about the only life they knew anymore, and they knew it well. A man didn't survive out here long without knowing the way of things. To them, each sound, each movement, had meaning.

Alexander Campbell eased his horse into the small mountain clearing and stopped cold when he saw the little camp. He suddenly suspected that he had stumbled into an Indian camp, and fear struck deep into his guts. He remained there, on his horse, unmoving, waiting for an arrow to strike him at any moment.

He was mighty hungry, and the smell of coffee and roasting buffalo meat drifting over from the fire sure was tempting. He saw no one around, and since he had not been shot yet, he figured it was not an Indian camp. Of course, he couldn't be sure, but he just had to have some of that food. He urged the horse slowly forward, toward the fire.

He froze again, fear renewed when he heard a voice coming out of nowhere.

"Hold it right there, boy," Finch had called, "or I'll drop ye whar ye stand."

The young man sat outwardly calm, clutching the reins of his horse as well as the lines to two pack mules. Those animals had only empty pack saddles on them. A rifle was held loosely in the crook of his left arm. He was frightened but trying not to show it.

"Light and tie, boy," Finch said evenly. "Then put your weapons on the ground where I can see 'em."

"I dunna mean no harm to ye nor anyone," Campbell said, wrapping the lines to the empty pack mules around the horn of his saddle. "Dunna go getting hasty in shooting." His burr was thick; his r's rolled.

"I jist ain't aimin' to take any chances, boy," Finch offered. "Ye do like I says and no harm'll come to ye."

Gingerly dismounting, Campbell let the reins dangle. He knew the horse would stay put. He looked around, but could see nothing. That annoyed and worried him. It was still daylight, and not being able to locate the speaker was an odd feeling. He gently laid his flintlock rifle on the short bluegrass. He pulled a big flintlock pistol from his belt and placed it next to the rifle.

"All of 'em," Finch ordered.

Campbell pulled out the heavy, thick-bladed knife from the hard-leather sheath and dropped it next to the others.

"Now step away from 'em." When Campbell had complied, Finch asked, "Ye alone, boy?"

"Aye."

As soon as he had seen Campbell enter the meadow, Sharp had slipped away and made another check of the area. "Ain't nobody else with that critter," he reported now.

The two trappers stepped warily from behind the bush, startling Campbell. "What's your name, boy?" Finch asked.

"Alexander Campbell."

Finch took a good look at the young man. He was a big, well-built fellow. Maybe not quite as tall or broad-shouldered as Sharp, but he still had some filling out to go. He did not look soft, though, which Finch figured was a point in Campbell's favor. The newcomer was pale, too, compared with Finch and his longtime partner. Where their faces and hands were toughened and weathered by harsh mountain winters, brutal prairie summers, by wind and rain, Campbell was purely white, the skin of his face soft and uncreased. Yet the mane of long, lank red hair and matching eyebrows, plus the cold, almost icy blue eyes gave him something of a wild look.

Campbell was dressed differently than the two mountain men, too. They wore faded, greasy, worn buckskin pants and loose buckskin war shirts, while Campbell wore heavy woolen pants. Finch figured they must itch like the devil during the hot weather. Campbell's shirt was of well-woven cotton, with tight cuffs and billowing sleeves. Big, square-toed leather boots covered his feet, and a flat cap topped his head.

"I'm Caleb Finch," Finch said. "This here's my partner, Ethan Sharp. Ye mind tellin' us just what'n hell you're doin' stumblin' around out here all by your lonesome?"

"It seems," Campbell said dryly, "that I've lost my way."

"No shit," Sharp said sarcastically. "What're ye doin' up in these parts in the fust place anyway?"

"I've come to join in the fur trade," Campbell responded evenly.

Finch and Sharp suddenly laughed. "Ye have, have ye?" Finch said. "Ye don't seem quite fitted for such doin's."

"Ye have no call to mock me, sir," Campbell said with wounded dignity. "I dinna make fun of ye." He looked at his two "hosts." They were a tough, competent-looking pair.

At about five-foot-ten, Finch was some inches shorter than Sharp, but he made up for it in bulk. While

Sharp was broad of shoulder and slim of waist, Finch was wide of both, but there was no fat on the broad, hard-packed stomach. Finch had short, powerful legs and arms, a bull neck and square head. His nose was splayed and flat. His beard and his hair, the latter tumbling out from under an animal-skin hat, were dark brown and thick. He had a small, crescent-shaped scar under his left eye. Oddly, his eyes were hazel, and seemed almost out of place in the dark face encircled by his dark hair and beard. The hands holding the short, heavy-barreled flintlock rifle were massive and brawny. Campbell decided then and there that he would not want to tangle with this bear of a man.

Sharp was a shade under six-foot-two, with a mane of very fine, blond hair. A thick, nasty-looking scar tumbled out of his thin hair, cleaved one ashen eyebrow and ended halfway down the side of his nose. Once long and angular, it was knocked off-kilter a little. His face was thin, with something of a pointed jaw. His beard was blond and difficult to see in the sunlight. Faded eyes of an even deeper blue than Campbell's gazed steadily from under the pale lashes and eyebrows. He leaned on his rifle muzzle, allowing Campbell to see the large knuckles on Sharp's big hands, as well as the cuts, dents, and damages from a hundred hard-won brawls.

"Ye got no call to make fun of us, boy," Finch said. "It's jist . . . Aw, the hell with it. Ye hungry?"

"Aye." The eyes gave the truth to the simple statement.

"Well, then, boy, tie your horse over yonder with ours and set. We got us some fresh buffler ye can fill your meatbag with."

"Aye, that'd be a fine thing, lads." He hesitated, then asked, "Might I retrieve my arms?"

"Your what?" Sharp asked.

"My weapons."

"Ye ain't plannin' no deviltry agin us now, are ye, boy?" Finch demanded, though he did not seem angry.

"I dunna wish to harm no one." He paused. "Well, almost no one. And ye lads aren't among them."

"Have 'em back then, hoss," Sharp said.

"Thank ye." Campbell retrieved his weapons, then walked his animals over to where Finch and Sharp's were, and tied them off. He unsaddled his riding horse and tended it swiftly. With hunger eating at his belly, he quickly pulled the pack saddles off the mules and rubbed them down perfunctorily.

While Campbell was so occupied, Sharp and Finch went back to the fire and sat, rifles at their sides as usual.

"He's about the greenest chil' this ol' hoss has ever seen," Finch said. He threw some more buffalo meat on the fire to cook.

"Christ, I think he's worse'n we was," Sharp said with a laugh.

"Shit, I don't know if anybody could be that bad," Finch rejoined.

Campbell returned and sat, like the others, cross-legged at the fire. Though it was still summer, there was a distinct chill in the late afternoon breeze. Campbell rubbed his hands in front of the fire. "Well," he finally said after building up his courage a little, "what're ye two lads doon out here?"

"We're free trappers," Finch said. "The cocks of the walk, by Christ. We're each of us half goddamn panther and half goddamn buffler bull. We're so god-damn fearsome, even the mighty goddamn Blackfeet fear us more'n anything that walks, crawls, or flies. Gros Ventres step out of our way, and Crows cower in their lodges when we pass by. We . . . " He was hav-ing trouble keeping his laughter bottled up.

Sharp was already laughing, and he finished up for his partner: "And we're full of buffler shit, boy. Me and this ol' chil' over here are about the biggest liars this side of Independence. But don't ye let on about that to no one."

Campbell smiled, and then laughed. "Aye," he said, "I'll be believin' all of what ye say, and I'll nae tell your secret to no one."

"That's right nice of ye, boy," Finch said. He stabbed a piece of meat from the fire with his knife and held it out for Campbell. "Hyar now, boy, ye jist feast on that. There's plenty more where that come from, too, so's ye make sure your meatbag's well filled."

The young man nodded and eagerly wolfed down the hot, dripping meat, seared to a crisp on the outside, still half raw inside. "Ah, tongue," he said with a satis-fied nod. "The best of the buffalo."

"You've had it before?" Sharp asked, a little sur-prised.

"Aye. Not too often, but, aye."

Finch and Sharp grabbed slabs of meat for them-selves. They happily ripped off chunks with their teeth, heedless of the grease that dropped onto their shirts and smeared their beards.

Campbell kept gobbling down bolts of meat, until Finch laughed and asked, "When's the last time ye ate, boy?"

"Couple days ago, maybe. I dunna know for sure." Finally finished, Campbell wiped his face and hands on his shirt. He nodded thanks when Sharp handed him a buffalo bladder that the two trappers used as a canteen. He drank deeply of the warm, musty water.

"Ye got any whiskey on ye, Ethan?" Finch asked. "I thought I'd stuck a jug in amongst my possibles when we headed east, but either I didn't do it, or ye went and pilfered it."

"I'd nary do such a low thing, and ye goddamn well know it, hoss," Sharp said, unfazed. "But I reckon I'll not hold it agin ye. 'Course, I might not let ye sample my *awerdenty*, either." He grinned as he stood and headed toward the supplies. He returned carrying a small earthen jug. He sat, pulled the cork, and threw the jug over his arm so the neck and top of the jug rested on his right biceps. Tilting his head back, he took three long swallows, then smacked his lips. "Goddamn, but that shines with this ol' hoss," he said.

"Goddamn, give me that thing," Finch snapped, grabbing the jug. He took a long drink and then held it out toward Campbell. "Here, boy, have some of this. That'll help ye forgit about the long trip out here."

"Dunna mind if I do," Campbell said smoothly. He took the bottle and drank. He didn't down nearly as much as either Finch or Sharp had, but he didn't miss by much. He set the bottle down. "Sure has some mighty kick to it, lads," he said, not seeming any the worse for wear.

"Hell, I know that," Sharp snapped. "Now jist pass it back here so's this ol' hoss can wet his throat again. Three measly swallers ain't quite enough for this hoss."

"Hold your horses, mon," Campbell said. "I canna say I'm finished with swallowing just yet." He took another long drink.

Finch laughed. "I think ol' Alexander's got him some possibilities here, Ethan," he said. He took the jug.

Campbell smiled. "Aye, that I do. But you laddies can call me Alex." He paused a moment. "And ye can pass that jug back around this way once more."

Sharp did so, before filling and lighting his old clay pipe. Finch followed suit with the latter. Then all three men settled in. Campbell found it odd that he was so comfortable with these two men, considering he had just met them. And considering the experiences he had had lately. He was determined to remain wary, but he relaxed considerably.

"So, boy, how'd ye come to be way up hyar all alone?" Finch asked. He was the more outgoing and gregarious of the two longtime mountain men; more accepting of people and happenings. He had already taken a liking to the young newcomer and felt as if he should make Campbell feel welcome.

"Well, now, 'twould not be much of a story to the likes of ye two laddies."

"Shit," Sharp said, chuckling quietly, "tell it anyways. I've heard every story ol' crab-ass Caleb's got to tell."

Finch smiled, as did Campbell, who said, "Then perhaps I better tell it from the beginnin'."

"Would be a good idea," Sharp said dryly.

"I was born in the town of Kippen Smiddy nineteen years ago."

"Whar in hell's this Kippen Smiddy place?" Finch interjected.

"In Scotland."

BUCKSKINS AND BLOOD / 11

"No wonder he talks funny, Ethan," Finch said with a wink. Though he and Sharp knew several Scots, the two had been in the mountains so long now that about the only speech they ever heard was that of the mountain men, that strange patois of American, English, Appalachian, French, and Spanish. It was sometimes grating to the ear of a newcomer, but to the mountain men there was a lilting, almost lyrical quality about it.

"Leave the critter alone about the way he talks, Caleb," Sharp said easily. "He talks better'n ye do any how." He grinned at Campbell. "Go on, Alex," he added. "Keep tellin' it." Sharp was not as open with newcomers as Finch generally was, but he was not all that closed off from them either. He usually took longer to accept a person, but something about Alexander Campbell had gotten through to him. The young Scot had a quality about him that Sharp figured would suit the mountains.

"Aye, I'll do so, if that's what ye laddies want." When the two mountain men nodded, Campbell continued. "We were a poor family. Aye, mighty poor we were. Kippen Smiddy, bein' such the wee place that it is, didn't offer me much opportunity, and schoolin' was a sometimes thing. When I was but eight or nine, I suppose—still just a wee lad—me pap apprenticed me to a merchant. Had me runnin' messages, sweepin' floors and the like."

"Don't sound none too awful to me," Finch offered. "Hell, I was workin' on the farm when I were that age. My pa put us all to work soon's we was able."

Sharp kept silent. He, too, had been put to work as a child, but he didn't much care to talk about it. It was just the way he was.

"Aye, the work wasna hard, even for a wee one. But the merchant was a bully; a petty tyrant. He was of the feelin' that he owned me once me pap apprenticed me to him. It wasna easy for a wee lad, I can tell ye that. Always at his beck and call; ne'er time to play with the other laddies. I dinna expect a life of ease, free from want. Nae. Such a life is not for the likes of me. But I dinna expect a life of slavery neither. Me pap was a proud man, and I inherited that from him." He grinned a little. "Aye, a free-spirited little lad I was."

The jug was passed slowly around; fresh hunks of meat were kept roasting and were eaten as needed, and pipes were kept lit. Campbell had relaxed considerably. He had had some bad experiences with mountain men before, but Finch and Sharp seemed a different breed from those men for some reason. Plus he was speaking of something that came from his heart. He had never really spoken of these things to anyone before, but for some reason he could not fathom, he felt no discomfort about speaking of them now to these two strangers. It helped, he supposed, that the two mountain men were attentive to his words.

"By the time I was twelve or thirteen," Campbell went on, "I was already a strappin' lad, bigger than most of my mates. And the work had gotten harder as I grew, strengthenin' my muscles more than a wee bit. 'Twasn't till I was a couple years older, though, that old suet guts, as I was fond of referrin' to Mister MacDougall, finally went too far. I could put up with his boxin' my ears for askin' for thruppence more a month for all the work I was doin'. And I could put up with his other miserliness and his mean-spiritedness, too, but when he put his hands on me mam, he went too far for this laddie."

"He put his hands on your ma?" Finch asked, surprised and disgusted.

"Aye. Seein' as I was the eldest of the brood, me mam was still young. And a pretty lass she was, too. Aye. MacDougall's wife was an old harridan. A mean-tempered wench straight from the bowels of hell. Aye, that she was. So MacDougall thought he'd avail himself of me mam. Where he got the notion, I dunna know. I overheard him, though, tellin' her that he'd fire me if she didn't favor him. All the while, he was tryin' to run his hands over her." The anger flared now, even though almost six years had passed.

Campbell took a drink from the jug, allowing himself to calm down a little. "She said she'd think aboot it. She dinna know what else to do. When she left, I confronted MacDougall over it. Resortin' to his old ways, he told me to mind my own business, then tried boxin' my ears again, like he'd done so often. I'm afraid I dinna allow it this time. I ended up killin' him," he added without remorse.

"Seems the proper thing to be done under the circumstances, this ol' hoss'd say," Sharp said with a firm nod.

"Goddamn right," Finch agreed. "Ain't no woman should be treated in such a way to this chil's thinkin'."

Campbell took a short pull on the jug, which was almost empty, and passed it to Sharp. Then he stabbed a piece of meat from the fire and talked around his chewing of it. "My pap was none too happy aboot any of this, but he dinna find fault with what I'd done. But knowin' that the law'd be after me soon, we decided I'd better be gone. I said good-bye to me folks and left home. I made my way to Glasgow, where I wound up gettin' in the way of all the workmen there, till they got to be thinkin' they'd pitch me in the drink."

"Ye more'n likely deserved it, boy," Finch said with a laugh.

Campbell nodded and chuckled. "Aye, Caleb, I expect so. But one blustery old laddie took pity on my poor, starvin' soul and offered me tuppence a week to run a grog shop and fetch the mates some rum. With nothin' better to do with my time, and my belly cryin' out for some food, I accepted."

"Didn't drink none of that rum, did ye, boy?" Finch asked with a chuckle.

"Nae," Campbell said, laughing. "I dinna think of't at the time. After that, the men on the docks would give me a few pence now and again to run errands for them. Finally I started workin' alongside them. It was hard work, and often dangerous. But at least I was gettin' paid a man's wages."

Campbell stared silently into the fire for a bit, thinking back to those times. Though it had not been too many years ago, it seemed like a lifetime to him. Loading and unloading the ships had been brutal, backbreaking labor, but it allowed him to see things he never would have seen otherwise. Things from all over the world: spices from the Far East, gold and slaves from the Dark Continent, exotic foodstuffs from the Continent, barrels of whale oil and blubber from the stinking whaling ships, silks from India.

Mostly, though, he seemed to remember the things that had come from America: strange foods, the occasional red-skinned visitor, treated either as slave or as royalty, tobacco, and furs. The latter really got his attention—thick, plush beaver skins that would become fancy hats for the wealthy of Europe; rough buffalo hides used for blankets; yellowish, supple elk; bear hides to be made into rugs or coats; mountain lion; thick, sensual wolf furs.

He heard the talk, too. Talk of the riches that lay there just for the taking in the far western reaches of America. Of how animals could be turned into hard cash money; of how John Jacob Astor had arrived in that land with but pennies in his pocket and parlayed beaver furs into a fortune rivaling that of King Midas.

The possibility of adventure stirred him, fostered by the occasional sight of a rough-clad American trapper getting off a ship. The trappers were men who through their will, strength and perseverance had made the fur trade what it was. Many was the time he thought that such a life was the one for him.

The danger did not scare him. He had heard the stories of the feathered savages who ran wild in the American West. He discounted much of that talk, though, since he had seen some Indians get off the ships, and they had not impressed him. Besides, he was used to danger and sudden death. It seemed that hardly a day passed that a man wasn't killed on the docks, crushed by crates of goods or falling in the brackish water to drown. There were the grog shops, too, where the dock workers spent a considerable amount of their nonworking time guzzling rum and thick ale. Sailors from around the world would also frequent such places. With the liquor, gambling and prostitution, brawls were commonplace, as was death by gun, garrote, knife, blackjack, or broken bottle. Often death came during a robbery that would net little more than a few pence.

No, danger didn't scare Campbell. Not even the unknown scared him. Almost anything would be better than the squalid existence in which he had found himself. In Glasgow there was no hope of bettering himself, finding a decent woman, marrying and raising good children. Because of all this, he dreamt constantly of going to America, though he never really thought he would get the opportunity.

Another brawl led him to make the change, though. An English sailor had gotten drunk in one of the grog shops and had been spouting off about the ways things were in America. When Campbell—in his quest for ever more information about that place—had asked him some questions, the sailor had grown angry and ignored the youth.

Campbell patiently tried several times to get answers to his questions, but the sailor was having none of it, and had finally said nastily, "Go home, matey. A boy shouldn't be in such a place's this anyway."

The saloon fell silent as the men, most of them who knew Campbell, waited for his reaction. It was not long in coming.

Campbell pasted the sailor on the side of the head with a strong fist, knocking the sailor down. "Mind your tongue, laddie," Campbell said harshly. "All I was doon was askin' a few questions of ye, and not a one of them of a personal nature."

Someone grabbed Campbell from behind as the sailor stood. "I'll show ye a thing or two, matey," the sailor said as he slammed a punch into Campbell's stomach. It was immediately followed by another.

As the sailor drew back a little for another punch, Campbell kicked him in the groin. Then he planted his feet on the floor and shoved backward as hard as he could, driving his captor until the man's back smashed into the bar. The man groaned and released his grip on Campbell.

Campbell whirled and hammered the man—another English sailor, he saw—in the face twice. The man sagged, then dropped.

Campbell spun again just in time to have the first sailor slam into him. Campbell slipped in the old whiskey and ale on the floor and fell, with the sailor half atop him. Campbell jarred the sailor with a forearm to the nose, and the sailor rolled off him.

As Campbell and the seaman got up, the sailor grabbed a bottle from the bar. He smacked it against the edge of the bar to break it, but it took him three tries to do it. He grinned maliciously. "Aye, you're done for now, matey," the seaman said.

Campbell backed away, reaching into his pocket. He pulled out his large folding knife and opened it. "Don't be so sure, ye scoundrel," he said harshly.

"Here, here, that'll be enough of that, laddies," the bartender shouted. He emphasized his command by smacking a large club on the bar with a loud report. "I'll have no more of this."

Everyone stood still for a moment, then bystanders moved in to separate the three combatants. Moments later, the two English sailors huffily stalked out, and Campbell put his knife away.

The fight annoyed Campbell, and he could think of little else over the next several weeks. Thoughts of getting away to America—where he could find adventure along with the danger—were never far away, and he finally resolved that he would make the trip to America soon, somehow. He didn't know how, though, since he had no money for such a journey. Still, the lure of it pressed and prodded him until he could stand it no longer.

A month after the fight in the grog shop, Campbell

approached the captain of *The Highland Star*, one of the ships that sailed regularly between Glasgow and the American mainland. "I'd like to sail with ye on your next trip to the Americas, Captain," he said politely.

"Is that right, laddie?" Captain Duncan Montgomery countered.

"Aye, sir."

"Have ye passage?"

"Nae, sir. But I thought I might be taken on as a hand to make my fare."

"So ye think ye want the life of the sea, do ye, laddie?"

"Aye. I canna think of anythin' I'd like more," Campbell lied.

"Well, ye seem able-bodied enough, lad. We sail before the cock crows dawn after the morrow. Sign here."

Campbell scribbled his name, proud that he was able to do so.

"Just one thing, laddie," Montgomery cautioned. "I'll nae brook no lollygaggin' about when we're under sail. You'll work till ye drop and then work some more. And if ye can't keep up with the rest of the mates, ye'll be thrown overboard."

"Aye, sir," Campbell said with a shrug. He didn't figure life aboard a ship could be any harder or more dangerous than it was on the docks.

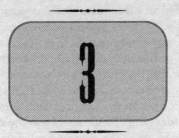

3

Campbell was wrong in his thinking. The docks were child's play compared to what he had to endure while asea. The days ran from eighteen to twenty hours, and since he had no other training, he and the few others like him were given all the work the trained seamen would not do. It was the dirtiest, most backbreaking, and most demeaning work he had ever done.

The first mate was a blustery, beefy-faced man who had little liking for his men. He had been at sea for more than thirty years, and had seen men like Alexander Campbell come and go. He hated them even more than his seamen, since they knew nothing and he considered them troublemakers at best. He made life for Campbell no more miserable than for any of the others in Campbell's position, but that was miserable enough indeed.

His "home" for the journey was a bunk area where he had an inadequate place to sleep and a few square feet to store his meager belongings. Food consisted of wormy meal and pork that was often infested with maggots. It was usually cooked into an evil-looking, fetid mush that turned one's stomach before it even reached the mouth. But it was all they had— with the rare exception of an occasional lemon or lime to prevent scurvy. The only relief was the daily ration of rum handed out to the men each evening.

The ship finally reached America, putting in at the busy port of Hampton, Virginia. Two days after docking, when the unloading had been finished, Campbell wandered up onto deck, a sack containing his few possessions in hand.

"And just where do ye think ye're goin' there, laddie?" the first mate bellowed. It was his usual way of speaking.

"I thought I might take some time ashore, sir," Campbell responded edgily. "Maybe see some of the city."

"Where the hell did ye e'er get such a notion, laddie?" the mate asked, sneering.

"I just thought . . . "

"Ye just get this straight, laddie. I'm the one who says who goes ashore and who don't, and when those that can go, go. And I dunna think ye'll be goin' ashore anytime soon, laddie. Nae. We set sail in the morn to return to Glasgow, and there's a plenty of work to be done aboard the *Highland Star*. And it's laddies like ye who'll be seein' to't."

"Aye, sir." Campbell's shoulders slumped and he dragged his feet below. He was angry, though, vowing silently, *I willna go back to Scotland now, not after reach-*

ing America. And they'll nae keep me on this ship. I'll nae become a seaman.

He planned to get off the Highland Star as soon as he was able to, and did not want anyone watching him with suspicion. So he worked long and hard, as he always did, throughout the day. When darkness came, he slipped away from the others below deck and grabbed his small canvas bag with his belongings. Moving quietly up to the stairs, he stopped at the hatch and looked out across the deck, until he spotted the first mate.

None of the regular sailors was on board, and the other men in his position had no love for the first mate. They would not betray him, he was certain. Captain Montgomery was in his cabin.

With a slight smile, Campbell crept forward, softly pulling a belaying pin from its notch in the ship's top rail. Without a sound, he crept forward and rapped the first mate hard across the back of the head with the sturdy wooden weapon.

He tossed the belaying pin to one of the men, who had grinned in appreciation, and then he hastened down the gangplank. Not sure where to go, he followed cobblestone streets until he found a tavern well away from the docks. He had little money on him, but he figured a real meal and a real bed were in order.

The next morning, broke but well-fed and rested, he set out on foot, heading north and west along the York River, and later the Mattaponi River. He found a ride twice over the next three days, when farmers came along and let him ride in the backs of their wagons for a spell. The second farmer, it turned out, was a Scotsman himself, and when he heard part of

Campbell's story, invited the young man to stay with him and his wife. Campbell agreed.

Campbell stayed with the Fraziers through the rest of the summer and for the long winter. He was mostly comfortable there, and enjoyed the old couple despite what he saw as their penuriousness. He ate well, and filled out somewhat, but the Fraziers were not nearly as generous with their cash as they were with their food. Over the long winter, Campbell realized that it was not so much stinginess on the part of the Fraziers. It was just that cash was hard to come by for anyone in these parts, and farmers, all of them, were loath to part with it.

He was glad to be some miles away from the docks, not wanting to run afoul of the *Highland Star* if she pulled into port again. Nor did he have any wish to be shanghaied out of some grog shop. He preferred the inns and taverns in Richmond, which were much nearer to the Fraziers' farm. He even met a serving girl in one of them.

Mollie Pruitt was not of Scots blood, but neither Campbell nor she cared a whit about that. Mollie's pert face, curvaceous body, and ready smile had Campbell about ready to plan on making his life in or near Richmond, Virginia. He didn't much like farming, but he figured he could put up with it for Mollie's sake—if he couldn't find another job in one of the towns in the vicinity.

There were things about Virginia, though, that didn't please him. After his confinement in the ship, the drudgery he had been forced to work at there, and the first mate's eagerness to keep him trapped on the ship, Campbell had taken a dim view of slavery once he saw it close up in Virginia. He didn't understand how men could treat others so, though he had no particular liking for those with black skin. Still, treating blacks so poorly went against his grain. Not that such a thing mattered all that much. He didn't have to stay in Virginia. There was no reason why he couldn't marry Mollie and move to New York or Philadelphia, or maybe all the way up to Boston and start a new life free from those distractions.

Others forced his hand before he was ready, though. It was barely spring when he was returning from Richmond. He had taken a load of crops into town for the Fraziers and spent a little time with Mollie and was making his slow way northeast back to the farm on the rolling hillside. That's when he spotted two men beating a slave. Actually, one was holding the slave, the other was beating him. The slave was not even as old as Campbell, and he was enduring a vicious drubbing from his white masters.

The man holding the slave youth looked up at Campbell. "Afternoon, friend," he said almost pleasantly.

Campbell stopped the small wagon. "What's goin' on here, laddies?" he asked, hoping he kept any anger out of his voice.

"Teachin' this buck nigger a few things," the man answered nonchalantly.

"Bein' a mite hard on him, aren't ye, laddies?" Campbell asked, still trying to fight down his anger. He felt nothing for the slave youth per se, but he could not bear seeing someone being treated so harshly.

The man stopped beating the youth and turned to stare at Campbell. "Y'all have a special fondness for darkies, boy?" he demanded.

"Nae, I canna say that," Campbell said easily.

"But that laddie's not gonna be of much good to ye after such a thrashin'."

"That's our lookout, boy," the man who was doing the beating said angrily. "Now go on about your business."

Campbell sighed and tied the reins around the wagon's brake handle. "Nae, lad, I canna do that," he said as he stepped down from the wagon.

Both other white men looked at him, their eyes wide in stunned surprise. They could not believe that any white man could object to the correction of a slave.

"Don't go mixin' in business that don't concern you, boy," one warned.

"I'm thinkin' that perhaps it's you two scoundrels who need some lessons."

The one holding the slave snorted. "And y'all think you're gonna teach us?" he asked sarcastically.

"Aye." Campbell was not afraid of these two men. Neither was nearly as big as he was, and both looked fairly soft. His only concern was if one or both had a pistol on him, underneath the suit jackets they wore.

The one flung the slave onto the ground. "We'll just see about that shit, y'all," he growled. He began reaching inside his coat.

Campbell did not hesitate. He took two steps forward and kicked the other man in the crotch. As the man doubled over with a red-faced whoosh, Campbell grabbed his hair, jerked his head up and smashed him in the face with a fist. Then he shoved the man hard.

The man stumbled backward, his face red and bloody. He crashed into his companion, and both fell.

Campbell slid out his large folding knife and

pulled open the five-inch blade. He moved in fast before his two opponents could get up and perhaps draw a pistol. He plunged the knife into one heart twice, and then the second. Then he wiped the blade off and closed it. As he walked toward the slave, he dropped the knife back into his pocket.

The slave looked at him with fear in his eyes. "What chu go'n do to me, massah?" he asked in terror as Campbell held out a hand to him.

"I'm not gonna do nothin' to ye, laddie," Campbell said, only a bit surprised.

Tentatively, the black youth took the hand and allowed himself to be pulled up. His dark face was already coloring up with bruises, and blood trickled from his nose and one corner of his lower lip.

"I dunna think I'd stay around here, laddie, was I you."

"What?" the slave asked dully. He still thought that this situation was incredibly unusual. After all, who would kill two masters over a slave? Unless . . . ? He suddenly was certain that Campbell planned to bring him back to his plantation to get a reward.

"I said, lad, that ye'd better get yourself a movin' before someone else comes along and tries to take ye back where'er ye came from."

"You mean run, massah?"

"Aye, lad. And I ain't your master. Nae."

The slave was almost certain that Campbell was going to shoot him in the back as soon as he ran, though he could not figure out why. Still, he turned and plodded off. Twenty yards away, he began to trot, shoulders hunched against the expected lead ball. A hundred yards away, he stopped and turned. He waved tentatively. He smiled with relief when

Campbell's voice drifted to him, "Good luck to ye, laddie."

Campbell looked over the carnage he had wrought and knew there'd be no end of trouble over it. It was too late to worry about that, though. He swiftly went to the two bodies and searched them. He came up with sixteen dollars and change, a pistol, small dagger, and a shooting bag. He shrugged and put the money in a pouch he wore on his belt. He put the other things on the wagon seat, climbed up and clucked the horses into an even trot.

Explaining everything to Douglas Frazier was harder than he had thought it would be, but Campbell stuck with it until it was told.

Frazier paced for a while, thinking, clouds of noxious smoke fuming up from his pipe to wreathe his head in malodorous clouds. Finally he stopped. "Maybe the authorities'll think the Negro did it," he said hopefully.

His wife, Mary, looked up at him. She was sitting at the table, mending a pair of pants. "Don't be a fool, Douglas Frazier," she said. "Maybe they will think that. But maybe they willna either. Then what? We sit here and wait for them to come and take young Mister Campbell away with them?"

"What do you suggest, then, Mrs. Frazier?" Frazier asked.

She stopped her sewing and looked at Campbell. "If I were ye, Mister Campbell, I'd go into Richmond and find that young lass you're so fond of. Then I'd take her and get away from here as fast as I could."

"Aye," Frazier agreed, seeing the intelligence of it straight off. "Aye. Ye can take our horse. Mrs. Frazier'll fix ye up with a bag of food to last ye a few days. Ye have the gun ye took off those men. Ye should be all right."

"Where do I go?" Campbell asked, annoyed at himself for ever having gotten involved in all this. No matter what happened, trouble was bound to follow.

"Head north, lad," Frazier said. "To Philadelphia or New York. Ye can lose yourself in the teemin' big city."

"Aye, I'll do't," Campbell said after only a moment's thought. "I'll head to Richmond now. I should be back afore long."

"Just make sure ye avoid that spot were ye did the damage," Frazier said.

Campbell nodded. "I'll take the more easterly road," he said.

He found Mollie in the Cotton King tavern, as he knew he would, and he beckoned her outside. "What is it?" she asked, annoyed. "Mister Reynolds won't be happy about this, if he should learn of it."

"Don't worry aboot that now, lass," Campbell said hastily. "How fast can ye gather ye things and be gone with me?"

"What?" Mollie asked, stunned.

"I've got to leave these parts, lass. Aye."

"But why?" Mollie was still befuddled.

Campbell explained quickly. "So ye see, lass, I've got to get away from here, lest the authorities come lookin' for me."

Mollie jerked her arm from Campbell's grip. "I'm shocked, sir," she said stiffly. "I couldn't go away with a man who'd done what you did. Kill two respectable white gentlemen for rightfully punishing a darky?"

"Ye mean ye'll not come with me, lass?" Campbell asked. It was his turn to be surprised.

"I will not," Mollie responded adamantly.

"But I thought we had . . . ?"

"We did. Until you fouled it with your foolishness. Now begone with you, Alex, before I call the authorities myself. I still might do so, but I expect I'll give you a little time to get on your way." She turned and huffed away as Campbell stood there dumbfounded.

"Shit," Campbell finally muttered. He turned and ran for the old horse. In half an hour, he was back at the Fraziers' farm, wolfing down baits of food. When he finished, Mrs. Frazier handed him two sacks.

"One has food for ye, laddie," she said. "The other's got a cook pot, coffeepot, and a change of clothes. I canna do much else for ye."

"Thank ye, ma'am," Campbell said. He kissed Mrs. Frazier on the cheek and then shook her husband's hand.

"Be gone now, lad," Frazier said sadly.

4

Within a few long days' ride, Campbell had found himself in Philadelphia. It was a bustling city, teeming with people and horses and carts and shouts and fights. He easily found the docks and got a job there doing what he had been doing in Glasgow. No questions were asked of him, and soon the bosses saw that he was a willing, hard worker who had done this work before.

The other men soon learned that he was affable and generally a pleasant fellow to be around—unless he was pushed too far. That was seen early on, as the men had to test the newcomer. Campbell had expected it and thought nothing odd the first time he was challenged by a hulking Swede who worked alongside him at the docks. Campbell hadn't won the fight, but he had gotten in some good licks and never gave up. The other men accepted him fully then.

The job gave him what he wanted most, except

29

for freedom—money; cash that he could use to realize his still-pressing dream of going west. There he would find his freedom, he thought. He saved what he could, finding cheap lodgings and eating as sparingly as his arduous work would permit. He spent less time in the foul taverns that lined the docks, choosing instead to hoard his slowly growing stack of coins.

He had it all planned out when he started working in Philadelphia. He would work there a year and a year only. Then he would leave. Toward that end, he sold the Fraziers' horse days after getting to Philadelphia. He had no need for the animal in town, and he did not want to pay for its keep in a stable somewhere. He felt a little bad about that, but he knew that if the Fraziers had expected to see their horse again, they never would have given it to him in the first place.

He worked all he could, too. Not only for the money, but also because he thought it would help him to forget Mollie Pruitt. The hard work served its purpose, but not nearly so well as he might've hoped. Forgetting her was made a little easier by his remembrance of her reaction to his news. That look of recoil and horror made it easier to realize that a union between them would never have been made in heaven anyway.

A year and three days after arriving in Philadelphia, he collected his pay and told his boss, George Holm, "I'll not be back on the morrow. Or e'er again."

"What?" Holm asked, stunned. It was not often that he found a worker like Campbell, and he hated to lose such a man.

"I said I'll not be back to work here," Campbell explained patiently.

"What's the matter, boy? Ain't we payin' you enough? Maybe I can get you a little more."

"The pay's fine, Mister Holm. But I need to be movin' on. 'Tis to the West I be headin'.'"

"Ain't nothin' out there but savages, boy," Holm growled. "Wild redskins and wilder animals." He could tell right off, though, that he wasn't frightening Campbell.

"I'll take my chances with the beasties out there, Mister Holm. Two legged or four. It dunna matter."

Later that day he left Philadelphia, heading west, riding a horse he had bought with his own hard-earned cash. He had little else, but he figured he was outfitted enough to find some of the wild places of the West and trap some animals. That would give him more money to outfit himself better, he figured. For now, though, he had his old cook pot and coffeepot, the pistol he had taken from one of the men he had killed in Virginia, an old rifle bought in a pawnshop, a bedroll, a sack of food, a small poke of money, and a tattered oilcloth pullover that he had gotten while at sea. He thought himself the king of the world, in some ways. He was free, on his own. He had no one and nothing to hold him back.

Somewhere in the rolling hills of central Pennsylvania, though, Campbell was bushwhacked by three men, who stole everything he had but the clothes he was wearing and the worn, weatherproof poncho, and even those had seemed in danger for a few moments.

He woke with a severe headache and a consider-able number of bumps and bruises. "Shit," he muttered as he stood there feeling sorry for himself. He could not believe the sorry luck he had. Then he shook his head. "Goddamn, laddie, don't ye go mulin' about how bad off ye are. There's a many worse folks in the world. Aye, 'tis not a pleasant thing to have happened, but we can make do."

Broke, afoot and hungry, he limped off, shoulders squared proudly. A day later, he found a farm where he managed to get a meal in exchange for some work. He didn't want to stay on there, and they didn't ask, so he pushed on. Such farmsteads were his salvation, though. He came across a number of them, and only once was he turned away without a meal. Most times he would work a few hours in exchange for the food, but every once in a while, someone would rebuff his offer to work and instead just feed him. Twice, a farm family even sent him on his way with a sack of dried food that would last a day or two.

He lost track of time and so was not sure how long it was since he had been bushwhacked when he arrived in Pittsburgh. Getting there gave him hope, and he immediately found a job on the docks—it was not much different for being on freshwater river docks instead of seaport docks—and began all over again.

Once more he gave himself a one-year deadline, and he stuck with it. This time, though, when he left, he went by boat down the Ohio River. The trip down the Ohio was uneventful to the point of being boring. He finally volunteered to help out on the flatboat, an offer that was readily accepted. He took a steamship up the Mississippi River when he got there, and alit in the town of Saint Louis.

He had managed to save enough money to arm himself and equip himself about the same as before, and still had enough money left to buy a horse when he got to Saint Louis. He had heard that Saint Louis was the gateway to the wide West.

He had never seen anything quite like it. The docks were like those anywhere and populated by the same sort of men and women as any other. But the rest of the city! Buckskinned mountain men strutted up and down muddy streets. Soldiers swaggered around. There were a fair portion of French-speaking people about and many who spoke Spanish. He saw more nationalities of people here than he had in his whole life together. There were slaves, too, of course, seemingly receiving no better treatment here than they had in Virginia. But he was most intrigued by the Indians he saw. They were, for the most part, defeated Indians, ones who had been driven from their lands and subsisted by trying to trade beaver and wolf and buffalo hides for food. Too often they spent their money on whiskey instead, trying to drown out the humiliation that their lives had become. Campbell could see none of that, though. To him they were somewhat noble savages, creatures he had heard about and never really thought he would see close up.

He found new and exotic foods here, too. Dishes made of fish he had never heard of before. Spicy delights concocted by the Spanish. And buffalo meat, that rich, succulent meat that he had heard the mountain men and wild Indians subsisted on. He could see why after his first taste.

He quickly learned that if he wanted to join a group going west into the mountains, he would have better luck in Independence, a couple hundred miles up the Missouri River. That the town was on a big river pleased him, since it meant that much less riding across what he had heard would be open ground between here and the mountains. He took another steamship from Saint Louis to Independence.

There he found that most of the men—whether free trappers, traders or company men—had left long ago. Campbell was pondering what to do when he met up with four gruff free trappers who, over the course of a drink or two, invited Campbell to head west with them.

"And how come ye lads're still here when all others've gone long before?" Campbell asked suspiciously.

"Had business to tend to here," Simon Beesley said. Beesley was a tall, dangerous-looking man with greasy hair framing a gaunt face. He was a big fellow, but still seemed somehow seedy and furtive. He appeared to be the leader of the small group.

"Aren't ye worried aboot gettin' out to the mountains before the trappin' dries up?" Campbell was still skeptical.

"Shit," Beesley said with a snort. "You're one dumb bastard, ain't ya? No matter, though. You wanna go west this time of year, we're about your only goddamn choice. Ain't that right, boys?"

His three companions nodded.

Campbell looked at them and was not heartened. Archie Tompkins was a handsome young man with an easy smile. Still, there was something about him that Campbell didn't much take to, though he could not put a finger on it. Val Knebel was tall and rail-thin. His buckskins hung on him like rags, and he was missing almost all his teeth. He seemed to be in his sixties, which Campbell thought a mite old for running around in the mountains. Juan Acosta was a short, narrow-shouldered young man, whose face indicated a viciousness that was almost startling.

"I'll let ye laddies know on the morrow," Campbell

finally said. He got up and left, figuring to scour Independence to see if there were any way at all to get to the western mountains other than going with the four he had just met. He went to bed that night dejected. There seemed to be only two alternatives to going with the four—waiting in Independence until next year, or going by himself. Just before falling asleep, he decided he would take a chance with these men. His quest had already been put off a year, and his luck showed little sign of improving. There was no telling what could happen in a year here. And he knew it was foolish to go alone.

The next morning, he uneasily told Beesley that he would go with them. Then he went out and bought such supplies and equipment as he thought he might need. At Beesley's suggestion, he even bought two mules—for carrying supplies out, even though he didn't have that many, but more importantly, for bringing his beaver furs back. It was precious little, all in all, considering the cost and how little money he had. But with rifle, pistol, bedroll, extra powder and ball, some jerky, butcher knife, and six traps, he began to feel himself nearing his dream of becoming a trapper up in the high mountains of the west.

The company of the four on the trail was as unpleasant as it had been back in Independence, Campbell quickly found, but after the first few days, there was little he could do. He kept to himself as much as possible. Tompkins seemed to be at least somewhat friendly, though, and he and Campbell would often play euchre or monte on a blanket spread before the fire at night.

They saw no one on the trail for the first couple of weeks. Then they met up with Indians twice. These warriors looked somewhat more fearsome than the ones in Saint Louis had, but still, the trappers seemed unconcerned about them. Indeed, a little tobacco here and there generally bought them off, and there was no trouble.

They finally made the Platte River and began following it. Campbell had become accustomed to the trail by now, but he still did not really feel as if he were part of the group. The men—including Campbell—took turns hunting. Campbell burned a fair amount of powder the first few times, too nervous—or just plainly too poor a shot—to hit even something the size of a buffalo. He learned, though, and by the time they passed Chimney Rock, he was as good a shot as any of the other four.

Campbell also helped in making and breaking their small camp, but that was about all he did with the others. He tended his own horse, cooked his own food, saw to his own gear. Other than his card games with Tompkins, he might as well have been by himself, he thought on more than one occasion.

Despite his perfunctory comradeship with Tompkins, Campbell still did not trust the man. He learned why he didn't like him all that much after they had been on the trail almost a month. Campbell had lost steadily, and suspected Tompkins might be cheating. He finally spotted it one night and challenged Tompkins.

"This chil' don't take to bein' called no cheat, sonny boy," Tompkins growled, coming up with a knife in his hand.

"I dunna give a damn what ye think, ye pustulent

scoundrel," Campbell countered, also coming up with a knife. Though he had become a good rifle shot, Campbell was better with a knife. He felt more comfortable with one in hand. He had no fear of Tompkins.

The trapper charged, and Campbell braced himself. It was over in less than five seconds, since the mountain man had seriously underestimated the Scotsman. Campbell blocked Tompkins's initial knife thrust, jarred the trapper with a strong forearm and then plunged the blade of his knife home in Tompkins's chest three times.

Campbell stepped back and let Tompkins fall. He watched Beesley, Knebel, and Acosta warily, figuring they would not be too happy with the death of their longtime companion. None seemed concerned, as they continued to sit around the fire sipping coffee, watching.

Tompkins had landed in the fire, and Campbell bent, grabbed the back of the dead man's shirt and hauled him out of the flames. He dropped the body a few feet off.

Once more Campbell looked around, wondering. "You lads aren't mad at me for killin' Archie?" he finally asked.

"He was a schemin' sack of shit at the best of times," Beesley growled. "He ain't no loss. Especially since we got you to take his place."

Still not sure, Campbell nodded. He didn't sleep well that night, though, fearing that the others would wait for just such an opportunity to get revenge. No one bothered him, though.

Beesley and the others seemed no more concerned in the morning, and after eating and breaking camp, Beesley said to Campbell, "It's your turn huntin', boy."

"Nae, it's not. It's . . . " He shook his head. It would have been Tompkins's turn to hunt. "Damn."

"You killed him, boy, you got to live with the consequences," Beesley said with a shrug. "We'll meet ya by Independence Rock. It's a big hump of stone that rises up out of the middle of nowhere a half-day's ride or so up the river. Ya can't miss it."

Campbell nodded. Now that he thought about it, he didn't mind going out to do some hunting. It kept him away from the others. While they still seemed as if they were not bothered by Tompkins's death, Campbell remained suspicious of them. He even considered just riding on by himself, but he figured that would be foolish. He had no idea how to get to the mountains or where to go even if he found his way there. Plus there were yet many Indians to contend with, or so he had been told. He hadn't seen that many, but he still believed the stories. Beesley and the others told about tribes as numerous as blades of grass, and all of them more fierce than anything he had ever encountered before.

He mounted his dusty brown horse and rode out of camp, once more feeling free. He took his two mules with him, to use for packing the meat back to their new camp.

As he rode, Campbell wondered what would happen when they got to the mountains. He didn't think he could stand living with Beesley, Knebel, and Acosta for an entire year. Maybe, he thought, he would find some other trappers up there, ones who were friendlier.

Campbell rode southwest, eyes keeping a lookout for buffalo. He didn't really want to shoot any too soon, since then he'd have to rejoin the others. He also kept an eye out for Indians, though he suspected he would not see any.

In the early afternoon, he found a small herd of buffalo grazing. He stopped and calmly dropped two small cows. He butchered out the livers, kidneys, tongue, hump meat, and ribs from both. He wrapped the meat in pieces of the buffalo skin and loaded them on the mules. Cleaning his hands on the rough grass, he rode off. Before long, he found the meeting place. Beesley had been right—one could not miss the massive hump of barren rocks amid the sea of prairie.

Campbell stopped and made camp. The place was well-watered, and there was plenty of grass around. He assumed Beesley and the others would want to stay the night here, and so he thought he would have things ready. Not that he felt subservient to the others; it was just that he was not the kind of man to sit around doing nothing.

Campbell waited . . . and waited and waited. For two days there was no sign of Beesley and the others. He even climbed to the top of Independence Rock several times and scanned the countryside. He saw nothing. Not knowing whether the men had been killed by Indians, or had deliberately deserted him, he decided to set off west by himself. He figured he had come this far, he could not see turning back, not when there was a tantalizing hint now and then of the mountains yet far to the west.

"Waugh!" Sharp grunted. "You've seen starvin' times already, ol' coon. But I'd say your luck's changed now. Certain it has."

"How can ye say that?" Campbell asked, surprised.

"Ye made it all this way without gettin' your hair raised, for one thing."

"Hair raised?"

"Gittin' yourself scalped, boy. Havin' red devils put ye under. Goddamn, hoss, you come through land crawlin' with Sioux, Pawnee, and other such nasty critters. And ye nary had any troubles."

"Well, that much is true, I suppose. It was a wee bit disappointin', though, not really seein' any Indians."

"Disappointin'?" Finch said with a snort. "Ye was one goddamn lucky chil' there, boy."

Campbell smiled a little. "I've heard the tales of the fearsome Indians out here in these western lands," he said. "But I've seen little evidence of it so far, and

I'm beginnin' to think that's what they be—tales."

Finch took affront at that, but kept quiet a moment, thinking it over. If, as Campbell had said, he had not really seen many Indians—an unlikely but possible event—he probably would have a low opinion of Indian danger. He finally smiled. "Ye jist wait till ye face a goddamn screamin' war party of Bug's Boys or . . . "

"Bug's Boys?" Campbell looked perplexed.

"Blackfeet. Meanest fuckin' Indians you'll ary meet anywhere," Finch said.

Seeing the look on Finch's face, Campbell was inclined to believe him. He suppressed a shudder.

"What made ye want to come out here in the first place?" Sharp asked. "Ye jist lookin' for some adventure?"

"Nae." He paused. "Well, not just that anyway. I canna explain it. I just wanted to become a fur trapper. Like ye two lads."

Laughter bubbled up out of the two mountain men, while Campbell sat there bewildered and more than a little angry. "I dinna think the likes of ye'd be makin' fun of a lad just because he might not be used to your ways. I'm willin' to learn and to work hard to become good at it."

Around the laughter, Finch said, "We ain't laughin' at ye 'cause you're green, hoss. It's 'cause we think you're plumb *loco*."

"*Loco*?"

"Crazy," Sharp said patiently.

"But why?" Campbell was even more befuddled.

"Hell, boy, trappin' ain't no fun," Finch said, laughter having faded. "Stand around half the time up to your ass in freezin' goddamn water settin' or checkin' traps. The rest of the time, you're scrapin' hides or makin' meat or lookin' for beaver sign."

"And all the while," Sharp threw in, "ye got to keep your eyes peeled for red devils and bears and such."

"Then why do ye lads do it?" Campbell asked innocently.

"How the fuck should I know?" Finch growled. Then he grinned. "We got reason, boy," he added. "Once you've been in these here Stony Mountains a season and have done it, ye cain't go back. Damn, if it don't have a pull on a man. Worse'n a woman's attraction, I sometimes think." He winked at Campbell.

"Do ye have women?" Campbell asked. "I've heard lads like ye often take Indian women to wife."

"Hell yes, we do," Sharp said. "We're married into the Nay Percy tribe."

"Nay Percy?"

"French words," Sharp explained. "Mean Pierced Noses. I don't know where the hell the Frenchies come up with that name for 'em, since I ain't ary seen a Nay Percy with his nose pierced. They do raise damn good horses, though."

Campbell nodded. "Where are they? Your women, I mean?"

Finch wasn't sure that Campbell didn't have some ulterior motive for asking, but then he decided the young man didn't. He was too guileless for such scheming. "With their people," he said.

Campbell's eyes raised. "Is that usual?" he asked, uncertain if he should.

"For some, I expect," Sharp answered. He stretched out his long legs, easing the knots in his muscles. "Not for this coon, though. Nor for Caleb. Ye know of rendezvous, hoss?"

Campbell nodded. "Beesley and his men talked of it."

"Speakin' of them ol' boys," Finch interjected, "ye aim to go after 'em, don't ye?"

"Nae," Campbell said evenly.

"That don't shine with this coon," Finch said darkly.

"I dunna know what that means, lad, but if ye're sayin' that I'm a coward, we may come to blows. I be not afraid of ye two or anyone else. Know that for sure. But I canna see chasin' after men who probably were killed by Indians."

"They could've been," Finch said harshly. "But ye don't really believe that, do ye?"

"Nae, I don't," Campbell said firmly. "But I come to these mountains to be a trapper, not spend my days lookin' for men to kill. I'll say this to ye, though, sir: If I come across those scoundrels in these mountains, they'll pay with their lives. Ye can rest assured on that point."

"Good," Finch said with a sharp nod. "Cowards don't shine with this chil', and I'll not be travelin' with any."

Campbell's eyebrows rose in surprise. It was the first anyone had mentioned him traveling with Finch and Sharp. He wasn't sure how he felt about that, considering what he had gone through with Beesley's men. Still, he could tell right from the beginning that these two men were far different from his former traveling companions. They were hard, tough men, their speech crude, their ways rough, but they came across as fair-minded men. He thought it might not be so bad traveling with them. He decided then and there to accept—if Finch had been serious in his offhanded remark.

"Well, Mister Finch, I'll have a go with ye right here and now, if ye be needin' that to convince ye."

Finch laughed. "Nope. I'll take your word for it, boy."

Campbell nodded. "Now, ye two were tellin' me about your Indian wives."

"I was, wasn't I," Sharp noted. "Till ol' Caleb had to go start flappin' his gums, tryin' to stir up trouble."

"Ye goddamn clap-ridden ol' shit, ye weren't gonna test that coon's balls. One of us had to."

"I didn't," Sharp said. "It was ye who was all afeared of this here strappin' young buck." He grinned. "Anyways, as I was sayin' afore yon crab-ass interrupted, we usually go to the rendezvous. We bring our wives and young'ns with us. Their familes're usually there, too, so it's a good time for visitin' and such. We did so this year, too, and was leavin' rendezvous with the Nay Percy with a few friends of ours, when one of 'em took sick. Bad sick."

"Ye mind if I have another bite of meat?" Campbell asked.

Both Sharp and Finch shook their heads.

"We decided it'd be best if ol' Charlie got back to the settlements to get treatment. Didn't seem to be shit we could do for him out here. So we sent the women and young'ns on with their folks. Caleb and me, well we took ol' Charlie as fast as we could back toward the east, hopin' to catch the caravans headin' back before they got too far."

"It wasn't for Ethan's poky ass, we would've caught up to 'em this side of South Pass," Finch threw in. "As it was, we reached 'em between South Pass and Independence Rock."

"It must've been South Pass I came through," Campbell mused.

"I expect it was," Sharp said. "Easiest way up into these parts. Ye must've gone through there before the caravan, though, or they would've seen ye."

"I must have," Campbell agreed. "I kind of wandered some, not knowin' where I was goin'. Ye two must have gotten ahead of me while I was stumblin' around. I canna think of any other way it happened."

Sharp and Finch nodded. They all fell silent for a while, listening to the wind in the pines, the snapping of the fire, the soft shuffling of the horses and mules. Campbell closed his eyes. He was so tired and felt so comfortable here that he relaxed considerably.

Sharp looked at Finch. They had been together long enough to sometimes know what the other was thinking. Finch nodded. Sharp returned the gesture.

"What's your plans, boy?" Finch asked, looking at Campbell.

The young Scot snapped awake, shaking his head. "I dunna know what I'll do from here." He wanted to ask if he could ride along with his two new acquaintances, but he could not bring himself to do so.

"Well, me'n Ethan're headin' back up to Tall Clouds's village. That's where our families are. It wouldn't put this ol' coon out none was ye to ride along with us."

Campbell wasn't sure what he felt. His poor experiences with Beesley and the others were still too recent, and more than a speck of wariness remained in him. These two men could turn on him in an instant, though for some reason he didn't think that was likely. He looked at Sharp. "And ye, Mister Sharp? Do ye feel the same?"

"Yep."

"I dunna want to get in your way." He was still uncertain.

"Ye won't," Finch interjected. "Unless ye start actin' as big an ass as ol' Ethan there."

"If ye can put up with Caleb's horse shit, hoss, you'll do jist fine," Sharp said, ignoring his partner.

Campbell had to think about it only a moment. "Then I accept," he said. "And I promise, gentlemen, that I'll carry my weight around ye."

"Ye don't, boy," Finch warned, "and you're gonna face starvin' times a heap faster'n ye did last time."

6

The morning broke bright and with the beginnings of a warm cloudless day. Sharp was the first one up. Throwing some meat on the fire, he walked to the small, clear stream that rumbled down from high up in the mountains somewhere. He plunged his head full under the water, and then snapped it out, shaking the water from his long, thin blond hair and stubby beard like a puppy, clearing the fog of sleep and last night's whiskey from his head.

When Sharp got back to the fire, Finch and Campbell were up. Finch was heading for the stream.

Sharp looked down at Campbell, who was sitting by the fire. "How're ye feelin', hoss?" he asked.

"I dunna think I feel too well," Campbell said. He sat holding his head in his hands.

"Ain't used to *awerdenty*, are ye?" Sharp said with laugh.

47

"I dunna think it was the whiskey," Campbell said quietly. "I've had more than that many a time. I think it was being left alone out there for so long, and not eatin' well. Then, when I poured the whiskey in me, and ate more than I should have . . ."

"No matter," Sharp said sternly. "Ye best git to the stream and dunk. It'll help clear your head. We got us a heap of travelin' to do, and me'n Caleb ain't got the time nor inclination for tendin' some sick ol' hoss."

"Aye," Campbell said dispiritedly. He struggled to his feet and shuffled off, passing Finch on the way. He returned soon, and joined the other two men at the fire.

While they were eating, Sharp said, "It's gittin' late, Caleb. We'd best be on the trail."

"Gettin' itchy for somethin'?" Finch asked with a grin.

"Well now," Sharp drawled, "it's been a time since this ol' hoss was with Many Bells. Of course, ol' hoss, as little as ye like to hump Dancin' Feather, I can understand why you'd be in no hurry to get to Tall Clouds's village again."

"Those are your wives?" Campbell asked, not sure he wanted to be in the midst of such bantering right now.

"Yep," Sharp said.

"You said you have children, too?"

Sharp nodded. "I got a girl, six, and a boy, three. Spotted Calf and Otter."

"And ye, Mister Finch?" Campbell asked, turning somewhat brighter eyes on Finch.

"A son, White Hawk," Finch said flatly. He stood and walked away.

Campbell turned confused eyes on Sharp. "Did I say something wrong, sir?" he asked.

"He lost a chil' a few years back," Sharp said in a monotone. "It still ain't easy for him to think on it."

"I'm sorry," Campbell said, r's rolling more than usual.

"He'll get over it."

Campbell thought that awfully callous, but then figured that Sharp knew his partner a lot better than he did.

By the time they were riding out of the camp a half-hour later, Finch seemed to be back to his usual self, which Campbell had found already was mostly jovial.

Finch led the way out, followed by Campbell, who held the ropes to the several pack animals. Sharp, ever alert, brought up the rear as they rode the thin ribbon of trail northwestward.

The heat made them drowsy as the long day passed. They did not bother to stop for a midday meal; hard jerky was eaten in the saddle. By afternoon, the two trappers rode with eyes half shut, almost asleep. Despite their seeming inattentiveness, they were constantly alert. Every movement or sound was catalogued by them. It all had meaning, and they noted it all without seeming to do so. Death came quickly to those who were not vigilant.

As they rode, Campbell began to wonder a little more about the two men he was now traveling with. Unlike with Beesley and his men, Campbell had felt comfortable almost immediately with Sharp and Finch, but still they made him wonder. He looked at Finch's broad, muscular back ahead of him. The trapper rode loosely, though he appeared to have been born to ride on the back of a horse. The shirt's back was greasy and bloodstained, showing the effects of years of use. Despite that, Finch still cut an impressive figure.

Campbell was also impressed with Finch's horse—a big, powerful-looking animal with dark spots standing out boldly along the grayish white flesh of the rump. The tail was long and full, reaching almost to the ground, and the mane was long and silky. It was, Campbell thought, a horse to be proud of, and one a man could put his trust in.

When they hit a patch of trail wide enough to allow it, Campbell rode up alongside the mountain man. "You awake, Mister Finch?" he asked.

Finch slowly opened his eyes. "'Course I'm awake," he groused. "And call me Caleb. It don't shine with this ol' coon to be called 'mister.'"

"Aye, Caleb, I'll do so. May I ask ye a question?"

"Reckon so, ol' hoss." Like most mountain men, Finch was reticent about talking about his personal life. Mountain men got hours of pleasure sitting around fires yarning, but didn't like giving out information about themselves. More than one had, like Campbell, headed into the mountains after trouble with the law. However, Finch was open enough to answer some questions, and if a question was asked that he felt no call to answer, he would see that it was dropped.

"Where'd ye get that fine-lookin' animal?" Campbell asked, pointing to Finch's horse.

"Like him?"

"Aye. And I canna say I've e'er seen another one like him."

"He's called an Appaloosa. The Nay Percy breed 'em. Ethan told ye yestidday they raise some mighty fine horses. This one was took by some Crows from a Nay Percy warrior named Far Bull, who was killed. A couple years later I counted coup on that goddamn

Crow and took this horse. I ain't ary had an animal quite like this one."

"What did ye mean by what ye said . . . countin' coup, I think ye said?"

"Yep, countin' coup." He perked up a little, seeing the opportunity to tell a tale perhaps. "It's somethin' all Indians do. Leastways all the ones this chil' knows of. To the Indians, there's more honor in gettin' close enough to an enemy to strike him with your hand or with a coup stick or anything else."

"They don't kill ye first?" Campbell was stunned.

"Nope. Hell, it's more of an honor if they count coup on ye whilst you're tryin' to kill him."

"Sounds dangerous."

"Well, hell, boy, it is. That's why there's so many honors in it. It ain't hard killin' somebody with a bow or a rifle. But gittin' close enough to count coup, well, that's a whole other thing. 'Course, there are times when ye got to rub out the son of a bitch before ye count coup on him."

"Ye have to do that with the Crow ye got the horse from?"

"Yep."

"What happened?"

"Well, me and Ethan and some of the Nay Percy headed east from their village one time, figurin' to hunt buffalo."

Finch could remember it well. The small party of Nez Percé warriors and the two white men. Finch rode next to his closest friend among the Nez Percé— Stone Buffalo, the brother of his wife.

Stone Buffalo grew more and more uneasy after they had been on the trail a couple of weeks. Finally, he said, in Nez Percé, "I don't like it, my brother."

"Don't like what?"

"The emptiness. There should be many buffalo here, but there are none. And few elk."

Finch shrugged. "Maybe they jist moved on south or somethin' a little earlier this year. Don't seem no cause for alarm." He answered in his version of English. He and Stone Buffalo had no trouble understanding each other, even when one was talking in one language and the other in another.

"Maybe you're right." Stone Buffalo smiled weakly. "I'm acting like an old woman, seeing danger when there is none."

Stone Buffalo's instincts had been right, though. Before another hour had passed, they saw small specks on the horizon in the vast mountain valley.

"What do ye make of that, my friend?" Finch asked, pointing to the dark dots in the distance.

"Crows," Stone Buffalo said flatly. "A war party. Big war party. Maybe twenty of them."

"Think we can hold 'em off?" Finch asked, unconcerned despite being outnumbered a little by the Crows.

"We aren't afraid of the Crows. They're cowards," Stone Buffalo said scornfully.

"Well, hell, I know that, but there's a heap more of them than there are of us."

"We've faced greater numbers before." He trotted off to speak with his other warriors to devise a plan. Soon some of the Nez Percé were breaking off and riding away.

The Crows continued their steady trot, pushed on by their belief that this was their land and that the Nez Percé were trespassing. In turn, the Nez Percé rode steadily on, unhurried, unafraid.

As the two groups grew near, the leader of the

Crows—a short, handsome warrior with hair so long it splashed down over his pony's rump—let out a war whoop and kicked his horse into a run. The other Crows immediately followed suit.

The Nez Percé returned the war cries and pushed on a little faster, ready for the battle. The two groups met with a clash and a swirl of dust. Clods of earth flew up from the horses' hooves; blood mingled with the foam from sweating ponies.

Finch rode into the thick of the battle at Stone Buffalo's side. He had shoved his rifle away, knowing it would do no good at close range. He grabbed out a big flintlock pistol from a saddle holster and fired at one Crow from close range. The .54-caliber ball blew the warrior clear out of the saddle, smashing him to the ground where he disappeared in the dust and under the feet of the horses.

Finch veered to the right, out of the way of a pudgy, flat-faced Crow who tried to count coup on him. Whirling his horse, Finch snatched out his tomahawk. He swung the weapon with deadly efficiency, clearing a swath through the knot of battling warriors. He saw Sharp and a Crow going at each other, the warrior wielding a war club; Sharp with a pistol butt. In the moment Finch watched, Sharp brained the Crow, knocking him down.

Finch spotted a young Crow painted entirely in white, with red streaks on his chest and arms. The warrior sat tall and proud on a massive Appaloosa. Finch forced his way forward, working his way toward the broad-chested warrior on the big horse. He recognized the animal as the one taken a year or so ago from Far Bull. Finch was determined to have the horse for himself now.

The Crow turned and saw Finch, and their eyes locked. They raced toward each other. Finch slipped the rawhide thong at the base of his tomahawk's handle over his wrist, noting that the warrior carried a long, metal-tipped lance in his right hand. He wore a shield, painted with a horse and lightning, on his left arm.

As they neared, the Crow's lance flashed out and struck Finch across the right shoulder and chest, knocking him to the ground. Finch rolled to a stop, wondering that he hadn't been stepped on by a pony, as he had landed in a spot that seemed oddly empty of other combatants.

Finch pushed himself to his feet, angry at himself. "Ye son of a bitch," he growled low in his throat when he saw the warrior, still on his pony, facing him, smiling in derision. The Crow charged again, swinging his lance at Finch, knocking him to the ground once more.

The Indian charged a third time, but Finch was ready. As the lance bore down on his chest, he shifted out of the way a bit and grabbed the lance just behind the point. He jerked suddenly, pulling the Crow down onto the ground while the Appaloosa trotted off.

The Crow was up almost immediately, ripping a French trade tomahawk from his waist.

"That ain't gonna do ye no good, boy," Finch growled. "I aim to raise your hair."

The Crow spat. He understood what Finch had said, but he was unafraid of the blocky mountain man. He snarled something in Crow that Finch didn't understand but didn't like.

Finch moved in first, whipping the tomahawk out in front of him in a wide arc.

The warrior leaped backward, bringing his own

tomahawk down toward Finch's head. The trapper ducked out of the way. The Crow pressed his advantage, pushing Finch slowly backward.

Then Finch's foot hit a stone and he fell, landing on his back. The warrior crowed with his impending victory. He brought the narrow, almost delicate tomahawk up, ready for the kill.

As the Crow loomed over him, Finch jerked out one of his belt pistols and cranked the hammer back. He fired.

The force of the blast caught the Indian in the stomach and jerked him upward an inch or so. The warrior wore a look of shocked surprise. He fell, partly atop Finch, who shoved him roughly off.

Without much pride, but without remorse, Finch sliced off the Crow's long, raven mane. Then he looked around, and spotted the big Appaloosa standing nearby. The battle seemed to be winding down, as the Nez Percé who had ridden off before the fight had finally circled around and attacked the Crows from the flanks. Finch edged toward the horse. The animal whinnied, nervous.

"Jist be easy now, boy," Finch said in quiet, soothing tones. "Ye got nothin' to fear from this chil'."

The pony shuffled his feet, ready to bolt, but Finch's calm, strong voice held it. The trapper gingerly grasped the horsehair rope that served as a rein, and stepped up to pat the broad forehead and scratch between the two flickering ears. "I ain't gonna hurt ye none, boy," Finch said.

The horse snickered and nuzzled Finch. "That's a good feller," Finch said. With an easy leap, he jumped on the horse's back. The animal bolted. He was accustomed to having his Indian rider mount from the right side, and having Finch mount from the left unnerved him. Finch quickly brought the pony under control.

The horse had stood him in good stead for the past five years, carrying him unfalteringly through blizzards and brain-frying heat, across empty plains and through narrow mountain passes, across deserts and rivers. The animal had proven to be not only a good, strong, dependable horse, but a great war pony and buffalo runner, too.

7

They rode on in dreary monotony, mile after mile, each with his own thoughts. Finally, Finch pulled them into a small grove of trees along a tumbling, narrow stream. It did not take long to make their camp, and soon the last of their buffalo meat was roasting and coffee was boiling.

"We best be lookin' to make some meat tomorrow," Finch said as they ate. He didn't look at Campbell, but it was to the Scotsman that he had addressed his statement. Sharp did not need to be told something so obvious.

"Ye e'er eat anythin' but buffalo?" Campbell asked. He knew he should know the answer to this and most of the other questions he had asked about life out here in general. But Beesley and the others had taught him next to nothing, and he was still in the dark about so much.

"Certainly, boy," Finch said. "Buffler's the best. Plumb goddamn shines it does. Cain't go none better'n buffler. But elk shines, too. Mountain sheep're right tasty, but them goddamn critters is some hard ones to catch. Roasted dog's not bad, and beaver tail shines with this coon of a time."

Campbell looked a little pale. "Dog?" he asked. "Beaver tail?"

Finch chuckled. "Hell, yes, boy."

"Ye ain't foolin' me now, are ye?" Campbell asked. "Ye lads actually eat such things?"

Both Finch and Sharp were laughing now. "Why sure," Finch said. "Ye spend any time up in these here Rocky Mountains, you'll eat them things, too. And a heap more besides. Ye git hungry enough, boy, and you'll eat anything ye can catch."

"I dunna think I can imagine eatin' anything worse than dogs and beaver tails."

"Shit," Finch growled good-naturedly. "After that slop ye said ye ate on that goddamn boat, ye turn up your nose at fresh roasted pup? Bah! A man's got to have different things to make life shine, boy. Like warm buffler hearts and livers, eaten raw, fresh out of the carcass."

"Beesley and his men ate such things," Campbell acknowledged. "I ne'er had the gall to try them, though."

"Goddamn, boy," Finch said. "Ye need to have more gumption. There's a heap of things ye can eat that're right tasty. Fat bear meat shines with this chil'. We've et rabbit, otter, horse, mule, ye name it. Ain't that right, Ethan?"

"Damn right," Sharp said laconically. "Hell, we even ate snake once. Ye remember that time, Caleb, don't ye?" When Finch nodded, Sharp continued.

"We was plumb starvin' that time. Goddamn, if we weren't. Hadn't ate anything for real in six, mayhap seven days. We was trapped by a powerful snowstorm up in the Cascades. The horses was near done in and we were fixin' to eat them critters, but without horses, we would've been in even worse shape, so's we were kind of stallin'."

Campbell sat entranced.

"We was diggin' around under some brush, hopin' to find some roots to keep us goin' a while longer when we found us a nest of hibernatin' snakes. We didn't know what kind they were; still don't. But we didn't much give a shit. We just clubbed 'em all to death, skinned 'em, and ate 'em raw since there weren't much in the way of fire makin's around."

"How'd they taste?" Campbell asked, gulping a little. Even the slop fed him on the *Highland Star* sounded better than feeding on raw snakes.

"Cain't rightly say," Finch commented with a laugh. "We was so damned hungry we jist kind of swallered 'em down as quick's we could, so I cain't say we tasted 'em. But they kept us goin' another day or two, till we found us an ol' elk some wolves'd brought down in the snow. We scared them critters off and feasted on stringy ol' elk."

Campbell nodded. "Aye, I guess a man can eat anythin' if he gets the hunger in his belly bad enough."

"Well," Finch said, standing, "it's robe time for this ol' coon."

Morning broke cool and blustery, with a strong wind blowing in from the north. "Damn," Finch grumped as he rolled out of his heavy, warm buffalo robe, "we're gonna git us some rain afore long."

Sharp grunted and stood. "More'n likely a real

goddamn howler," he said. "This ol' hoss ain't lookin' forward to ridin' through it."

"Me neither," Finch noted as he knelt to build up the small fire.

Breakfast was a hurried affair, and quickly over. While they ate, though, Finch asked Campbell, "Ye got anything to wear to keep yourself dry and warm once the storm hits, boy?"

Campbell nodded. He went and got his tattered oilcloth poncho-type garment. It was about the only thing he really had left from his days at sea. "They used these on the ship," he said.

"Waugh," Finch grunted. "That scrawny piece of shit ain't gonna do ye the least bit of good out here, boy. It's full of holes and too goddamn thin to ward off the wind."

Campbell shrugged. "I dunna have anythin' else," he said.

"Ye still got that old buffler robe, don't ye, Caleb?" Sharp asked.

"I jist might," Finch said, standing. He went to their packs and rummaged around. "Goddamn, if I don't," he finally said, turning. He had a large buffalo robe in his hand. He grinned a little. "It ain't the best lookin' thing this coon ary seed, but it'll do," he noted. He draped the bulky thing over Campbell's shoulders. He tugged it this way and that, seating it as best he could. Then he pulled his big butcher knife from the belt scabbard and made a few quick, deft slices, the sharply honed blade gliding easily through the tough hide.

Finch stepped back a moment, checking out his handiwork. Then he jabbed the knife through the open front of the skin a few times, making holes on each side. He slid the knife away and jerked loose a few of the rawhide fringes from the outside seam of his pants. He slid the thongs through the holes and tied them. Then he pulled a flap of the buffalo skin over Campbell's head and tied that down with more fringes.

When Finch was done, Campbell was covered in thick buffalo hide, the shedding-hair side in, and a crudely fashioned hood covered his head. It was warm and would be virtually waterproof.

"Thar now, boy," Finch said, stepping back and smiling, "ye look jist dandy. Don't he, Ethan?"

"He looks like shit," Sharp said critically. "But at least he'll be warm and dry once the rain hits." Then he shrugged.

"I must look a sight," Campbell said, embarrassed.

Finch laughed. "Don't go gittin' so high and mighty, boy," he said. "Ye mightn't be the fanciest out-fitted critter this chil's ary seed, but when that storm hits, you'll be mighty glad ye got that there robe."

Campbell nodded and pulled the heavy thing off so he could finish his work.

They were on the trail barely an hour when the storm hit. It came hard and fast, with great torrents of icy rain pouring out of a black sky. Thunder cracked off the mountains, and long strings of lightning spat at the ground.

Just before the rain had started, Finch had stopped and pulled out his own buffalo robe and pulled it on. Campbell looked behind him and saw Sharp tugging on a woolen capote made in the Hudson Bay style. Campbell figured the two mountain men must know something, so he pulled on his own new, hastily fashioned coat. Minutes later the storm broke. Though hard rain and cold winds were nothing new to a man born in Scotland, he was certainly glad Finch had made the makeshift coat for him.

The rains eased in midafternoon, and an hour later, most of the clouds finally broke and fled. The air warmed rapidly, and dried out a little. The three men shucked their coats and basked in the sun, which still played peek-a-boo with the clouds that lingered.

A small herd of elk drifted by ahead of them, and Finch trotted back to Sharp. "Them elk'd make good meat," he said.

Sharp nodded. "I was thinkin' the same."

"Why don't ye go on off and make some meat, Ethan? Me'n Alex'll ride on up and find us a place to stay up along the Siskidee."

Sharp nodded. He cut out a mule and trotted off, heading west to move in on the elk herd.

"Ethan going to be all right by himself?" Campbell asked. "I thought it was dangerous out here."

"No more so than anywhere else."

"What about redskins?"

"Only ones to be worried about around hyar are Shoshones, and they're generally friendly." He paused. "I'd advise ye to watch, though, jist who you were callin' redskins. It wouldn't shine with neither me nor Ethan to have ye go callin' the Nay Percy redskins."

"I dinna mean no harm," Campbell said, surprised. "It just seems that e'eryone I've met has called Indians redskins—or somethin' similar."

They started riding again, heading northwest, the way they had been going.

"I know ye didn't mean no harm, boy. The trick is knowin' which Indians to call redskins."

"How do ye know?"

"Depends on them critters," Finch said with a smile. "I usually save such things for them that deserve it. Someone steals my horses or my plews or any of my plunder, well, he's a fuckin' red devil, and I aim to make that chil' pay."

Finch paused to stick some tobacco in his mouth and start chewing it. "Most of the mountaineers has got themselves tied to one tribe or another. As ye know by now, me'n Ethan deal with the Nay Percy. Ol' Gabe Bridger now, he's with the Shoshones. Bill Bent down in Mexico, he's partial to the Cheyennes. We all're friends with other tribes, too, but not so much as those ones for ourselves."

"Aye," Campbell said, acknowledging it. "But how do ye get linked to one tribe and not another?"

"Hell if I know," Finch responded. "It jist sort of works out that way." He knew that was an inadequate explanation, but it was the best he could do. "Ye watch over the animals," he growled as he trotted ahead. He felt discomfited at times like this. Despite his outgoingness and his love of talk and chatter, there were too many times he felt inadequate in trying to explain something. Like now. Often, he knew in his heart what he wanted to say, but the words would not come.

They found a good campsite about two hours later, and began doing their chores. The horses and mules had to be tended and turned out to graze, wood had to be gathered and a fire built.

They had just put coffee on to boil and sat down—Finch on an almost flat rock, Campbell on a log—when suddenly Finch's head snapped up, alert.

"What is it?" Campbell asked in a whisper. He was alarmed.

"Shet up," Finch growled. "Grab your rifle, and git behind that tree yonder." He pointed. "Then ye do jist what I tell ye."

"Aye," Campbell said, worried. He picked up his rifle and took refuge behind a cottonwood.

Finch stood in the clearing, senses seeking out whatever it was that had alerted him. Then he caught something out of the corner of his eye, and he relaxed. "C'mon out, Alex," he said. "It's only Ethan comin' in."

Campbell stepped out from behind the trees just as Sharp rode up.

Sharp nodded as he stopped and slid off his horse. "I'd be obliged if ye was to care for my horse and the mule whilst Caleb and I start roastin' meat, hoss," Sharp said to Campbell.

The Scotsman nodded and set down his rifle. When he got back to the fire, the meat was sizzling, smelling delicious. He squatted down. "Ye see any Indians while ye were out there, Ethan?" he asked.

"Nope. Was I supposed to?"

"Nae. I just . . ."

"He was worried about red devils findin' ye," Finch said with a laugh. "I was tryin' to explain to him that not all Indians is red devils, but I expect I didn't do such a good job of it."

"Ye nary was any damn good at explainin' things, even though your mouth is goin' all the time," Sharp said dryly.

"Then ye try it," Finch countered, unperturbed.

Sharp tested the meat with the point of his knife and found it not yet ready. "Look, hoss," he said, "Indians're people jist like the rest of us. There's good'ns and bad'ns. Some of 'em, like the Nay Percy, are good all the time. Leastways they are to me'n

Caleb. The Flatheads're the same, and most everybody usually gits along with the Shoshones, and the Crows, though they can be troublesome at times, especially for small groups."

"There's some that're bad all the time, too," Finch put in. "The Apaches down south, though me'n Ethan've nary dealt with them critters much. Same with the Kiowas and Comanches. But the ones that no white man I know've has got a likin' for are the Blackfeet. They're jist the plain meanest critters this chil's ary dealt with."

"Why's that?" Campbell asked.

Finch shrugged and reached for some meat. "I hear tell it was because of a trapper named John Colter. He traveled among the Crows back in 'ought-eight or so. Seems that whilst he was with 'em, they come on a Blackfoot war party and a fight commenced. Colter ended up killin' a Blackfoot. They ain't taken a shine to any white man since."

"That a true story?" Campbell asked flatly. "Or a tale?"

"I ain't sure. All I know is that the Blackfeet ain't to be messed with, and that those red devils come down hard on any white man they see."

8

"How'd you two get so friendly with the Nay Percy?" Campbell asked as they all dug into the elk meat.

"Well, now, it were a time ago. Ye remember it, Ethan?" Finch said.

Sharp nodded and reached into the fire for some more meat.

"Ye want to tell it?" Finch's eyes glittered.

"Hell, hoss, you're the one with the gums flappin' all the time. Ye tell it."

"Well, let's see," Finch said, unoffended, "it were back in, what, 'twenty-six, Ethan?"

Sharp nodded.

"Ethan and I met when we came to the mountains with a supply caravan headin' for the rendezvous. It was the first time rendezvous'd been held, but you'd nary know it. Goddamn was them some shinin' doin's. Once we'd seen that, we had us a powerful hankerin' to stay in these mountains and become trappers like so many of those we'd seen there at rendezvous. Before them doin's was over, we'd signed on with a few free trappers."

Finch grinned and took some meat. "A chil' named Tom Skinner was elected leader of the small group. We stuck with Skinner and his men for two years before headin' out on our own. By then, Skinner had introduced us to the Nay Percy, and me'n Ethan had us women in the tribe. We was welcomed by those people, and so we consider 'em our brothers now."

"Aye," Campbell said, "I can understand that." He paused. "Do ye think they'll take me in the same way?"

"Sure," Finch said matter-of-factly. "The Nay Percy are good folks. Open and warm of heart. But let me warn ye this, boy," Finch added harshly. "Don't ye ary cross 'em, or I'll have your hair hangin' from my lodgepole."

"I dunna have nae desire to anger your friends. But from what I've heard, I'll ne'er understand them."

"Most white folks don't. That's why there's so much trouble between us. Most of us trappers don't even fully understand 'em, even though we live with 'em as often as not. We understand 'em better'n most folks, maybe, but still, not all that well. All Indians got strange ways, boy—strange ways to us. But most of us boys accept Indian ways, even if we don't believe in 'em. That's why we can git along with most Indians, even if we ain't exactly friendly with 'em."

"Wha' do ye mean?"

"Well, I ain't got much love for the Crows, but I can generally trade with 'em if'n I have to. Same with the Utes. Still, don't mean I trust 'em. Bastards'll steal anything they can put their hands on. Especially the goddamn Crows." Finch shrugged. "But that's jist their way. Indians jist look at things different than we do."

They drifted off to sleep soon after and got another early start on a cloudless, warm day. During the ride that day—and continuing each day thereafter—Finch began showing Campbell the things the youth would need to survive out in this harsh, unforgiving land. On occasions, the more laconic Sharp would lend his expertise to the enterprise.

For his part, Campbell was astute enough to know how green he was. He was even angry that Beesley and the others had taught him absolutely nothing about any of these things. He was grateful for the tutoring given by Finch and Sharp. He proved to be a good student, looking, listening, and learning. He asked plenty of questions and accepted their answers; at first, always at face value, but later with more discrimination. The two mountain men were fond of pranks and, like most of their kind, were prone to stretching the truth when it suited their purposes. Campbell had soon learned to tell when Finch and Sharp were telling the truth, for the most part, and good-naturedly joshed them about their fabrications.

Some of the things he had the hardest time swallowing were the tales of the men and places in the mountains. Stories like that of Hugh Glass, or Jim Bridger's mountain of mirrored glass, or Black Harris's "putrefied forest," or Colter's Hell, or the giant lake of salt water, like that of the great ocean he had crossed. In time, he would see many of these places for himself, and come to believe in them.

Finch and Sharp were a little surprised at Campbell's prowess with hunting, considering that he was using an old, worn rifle. But while he was a good shot, the rifle often betrayed him.

"We aim to fix ye up with a real rifle soon's we can," Finch said one day after Campbell had missed a long shot at an elk. "Then you'll shine, boy. Plumb shine."

"But I have nae money for a new rifle," Campbell said quietly.

"We'll start trappin' soon. Afore long you'll have more'n enough plews to buy ye a good rifle, one that shoots plumb center ever' time."

One day they spotted a small herd of buffalo. Finch called to Sharp, who trotted up. He nodded when Finch pointed, but asked, "Ye think ol' hoss over there's ready?"

"Ready for what?" Campbell interjected.

"Runnin' buffler, boy," Finch said with a grin.

"Doon what?"

"Jist nary ye mind. Ye jist follow me'n Ethan." He started riding slowly off. "I only hope that horse of yourn's a good one."

"He's a fine animal," Campbell said a little defensively.

"He best be, boy," Finch said with a laugh, "or you'll get yourself killed."

Minutes later, they stopped at a stand of trees downwind of the buffalo, and they tied their pack animals off. Then they rode on, staying downwind of the grazing beasts, which paid the men no heed. When they were within twenty-five yards of the herd, Finch stopped. "Ye do what we do, boy," he said to Campbell. Then he let out a whoop that was echoed by Sharp.

Both men shoved a handful of lead rifle balls in their mouths before racing toward the animals. The buffalo started lumbering away, startled by the noise, and quickly picked up speed.

Finch picked out a fat cow and sent his Appaloosa charging after the animal. Within moments he pulled up alongside the bison's right side. He looped his reins around the saddle horn. The Appaloosa needed no guidance. Finch flipped the rifle down until the muzzle almost touched the buffalo's shaggy side. Then he fired.

The buffalo bellowed and went sprawling on its chin, its spindly legs unable to bear its weight.

The Appaloosa raced on as Finch raised the rifle. He blew into the muzzle and then poured some powder into it. He spat one of the lead balls into the muzzle and jammed it home with the wiping stick, fast and hard, and he was ready again. He carried the rifle muzzle upward so the ball would not fall out.

Thundering along in Finch's wake, Campbell had watched in amazement. He knew he had to try it now, once he had seen it done. Spotting a small bull to the side of the herd, he angled toward it and soon was pounding along beside the great beast. He brought his rifle down, as he had seen Finch do, and fired.

The bull roared and staggered a few steps. Then he caught his pace again and kept running. Campbell was trying to reload as he had seen Finch do while his horse continued barreling along beside the buffalo. The bison suddenly swung its horned head around, narrowly missing the horse.

Campbell's eyes widened in fear and awe, but he kept up his dogged pursuit of the bison. Finished reloading, he got some priming powder into the pan, snapped the frizzen shut and fired again. The bull fell this time, blood spurting from nose and mouth.

Campbell beamed in joy, almost stopping in his excitement. He would have whooped were it not for the mouthful of rifle balls. Then he raced on again, trying to catch up to the herd. *Aye*, he thought, *this be the life*. It was like nothing he had ever experienced.

More confident now, he charged toward an imposing bull, a massive block of an animal. As he pulled alongside and fired, though, the beast swung his huge head. The movement threw Campbell's shot off, and the ball only grazed the buffalo, enraging it.

The bull shifted slightly to the side, bumping Campbell's horse hard. The pony squealed in pain, and its legs buckled, pitching Campbell over its head.

The Scotsman bounced hard, grunting with the pain of suddenly bruised muscles, but he kept his grip on his rifle. As he scrambled up, he saw that his horse had recovered and was racing off.

The big bull had stopped some yards away and turned toward Campbell. The animal snorted and then charged.

"Jesus," Campbell muttered as he furiously tried to reload his rifle. When he did, he settled on one knee to steady himself, remembering the advice Sharp had given him a few days earlier: "Ye ary have to face a buffler head on, hoss, shoot for the chest. Ye hit that critter in the head and all you'll do is get yourself stomped into the ground. A buffler's head is the hardest kind of thing, this chil's sayin' to ye."

Heart in his throat, Campbell forced himself to wait as long as possible, wanting to get off as good a shot as he could, considering he was only going to get one. At last he fired, but the buffalo kept coming.

The bison finally went down a few feet later, sliding along on his chin whiskers.

"Dear mother of Christ," Campbell breathed as he shoved to his feet and then jumped. The buffalo carcass slid under him, and he came down atop it, twisting an ankle a little and falling off to the side. He scrambled up, heart pounding, but saw that the buffalo was dead.

Campbell sat with a plop, stunned, looking at the great creature.

He was still sitting that way a few minutes later when Sharp, and then Finch, rode up. "What the hell's wrong with ye, boy?" Finch asked.

Campbell staggered to his feet and looked around, eyes still dazed. He said nothing.

"Well, c'mon, boy, tell it," Finch ordered with an understanding grin.

Campbell seemed not to hear, so Sharp said, "That thar bull was about to ground our *amigo* into Mother Earth. Ol' hoss missed his fust shot and the bull knocked his horse ass over teapot. Goddamn, but ol' hoss went sailin'. Looked like the great Thunderbird." Sharp laughed.

Finch joined in the laughter and asked, "That true, boy?"

Campbell shook himself out of his fog a little. "I dunna know what this great Thunderbird is," he said slowly, "but I do know I felt like some kind of bird flyin' through the air. Aye." He rubbed his back and rear end. "Had a hard landin', too."

"Then what happened?" Finch asked.

Seeing the youth was still shook up, Sharp said, "After ol' hoss landed, that bull gave him the eye, all set to finish him off. But ol' Alex thar, he weren't about to be put under so easy. Cool as could be he loaded that ol' rifle of his and waited. Then he kilt that ol' bull."

"Shit, ye expect me to believe such a goddamn tale?" Finch said with a laugh.

"Shot him plumb center," Sharp said. "'Course, I think he waited a mite too long, seein's how the damn bull near run him over even after he was shot." He laughed some more.

"Well, I'll be damned," Finch said, a note of admiration in his voice. "Ye sure made 'em come now, boy. Goddamn, if'n ye didn't."

Campbell flushed a little, but threw out his chest in newfound pride. "There was nothin' to it," he said in false modesty. "Aye, that's a fact." He grinned. "Especially since I dinna know what else to do."

Finch whooped and did an impromptu little dance. "You'll do, boy," he say. "Goddamn, if'n ye won't." Still grinning, he said, "Now we best make us some meat."

A few weeks later, Campbell could sense a change in his two companions. He rode up and asked Finch about it.

"We're gittin' close to the village," Finch answered, and it was obvious to Campbell that he was looking forward to getting there.

"When'll we be there?" Campbell asked, feeling a quickening of his pulse.

"Tomorrow. Mayhap the next day."

Early the next afternoon, Finch called Campbell and pointed to the ground. "What do ye see, boy?" he asked.

"Indian sign?"

"Yep. See how the grass is worn down like there's a heap of horses been here not long ago? Plenty of fresh horse droppin's, too. Not much game to be seen. It's been run off or killed already." He pointed again. "Plenty of buzzards and ravens and such up there. A sure sign there's an Indian village around nearby."

Sharp trotted up. "I figure it ain't more'n a mile or two."

Finch nodded.

They rode on and soon topped a small rise. The camp was spread out ahead of them. "There it is, boy," Finch said.

"How can you tell it's the right village?" Campbell asked. From what he had learned, Indians generally lived in fairly small bands, only getting together in larger groups now and again for ceremonies. It made sense, considering the number of horses most of the western Indians had. Trying to keep the area clean, finding enough forage for the horse, having enough game around, all conspired to create small villages.

"See that one lodge there with the bufflers painted all 'round it?" Finch asked. When Campbell nodded, Finch said, "That's Stands in the Water's lodge. He's my wife's pa."

9

Campbell was distinctly uncomfortable and felt decidedly out of place as he moved amid the lodges and meat racks and red faces of the Nez Percé village while his two companions greeted friends and family alike. It did give him a chance to look over the people of the village, though.

The Nez Percé were, Campbell found, a handsome people, fairly tall and generally thin. They had dark, expressive eyes over long, strong noses. The men carried themselves with dignity and straight bearing. The women were not as subservient as he had thought they would be. They were attractive for the most part, with high cheekbones, smooth dusky skin and open countenances.

Most of the men wore their hair loose about their shoulders, though a few had two braids. Almost all had the front of the hair combed up into something of a crown that was stiffened with grease. A few had a rectangular patch of hair down the center of the forehead, almost to the bridge of the nose. They generally wore long, loose buckskin shirts, heavily fringed and decorated with beads and shells; leggings of buckskin or blanket material, also decorated; breechcloths of either material; and simple, soft moccasins.

The women wore their hair loose or braided, there seemed to be no standard. Their dresses were long and had extra buckskin material forming an additional yoke to the dress. This extra yoke was heavily adorned with glass beads, dentalium, bits of metal, and fringes. They wore leggings and moccasins.

Campbell was a little surprised when he saw Finch and Sharp stop in front of a lodge, where an old man was standing. Campbell had been sure the two mountain men would go straight to their women. Campbell stopped, too, and whispered to Sharp, who was closer to him than Finch was, "Who's that?" He pointed to the old man.

"The principal chief of the village. Civil chief. His name's Tall Clouds."

Campbell looked him over. The warrior was very old, his hair mostly white. But he still held himself straight and with dignity. A few eagle feathers in his hair fluttered with the breeze, and he had a heavy, four-point Hudson Bay blanket around him, held with his left hand at just above midsection, leaving his right arm free to help him communicate.

"I thought you and Caleb said the Indians don't have one chief."

"They don't. Now shet up."

Finch spoke to Tall Clouds in Nez Percé, while Sharp translated for Campbell: "My Father, it is good to be back among the Real People. I hope your journey was free of troubles and that food was plentiful."

Tall Clouds answered in kind, welcoming Finch and Sharp back to the village. "There were no troubles on the trail," he then said. "Except those brought about by an old man's infirmities."

"Hah!" Finch snorted. "You'll outlive us all, old man." He grinned.

Tall Clouds returned the smile. "We will feast tonight," he announced loudly to all who were assembled. "And dance. We must welcome our brothers back properly."

Campbell once more followed along, extremely conscious of the Nez Percé's eyes on him, as Finch and Sharp walked off, towing their horses behind them. Campbell had the pack mules. They came to two lodges next to each other but set off a little way from the rest. A young woman was standing outside each one. With one woman were two children; with the other, only one.

Finch headed for the latter; Sharp the former. Campbell stood there feeling like an absolute fool, not knowing what to do. He felt even more awkward when his two friends disappeared into the lodges with the women. So he stood there holding the ropes to the mules and his horse, trying to seem nonchalant while Nez Percé men, women and children edged closer to him. He wondered why that was; obviously, he was not the first white man they had seen.

A boy of about four finally gathered his courage and came right up to Campbell. The boy looked up at the towering Scotsman, then indicated that Campbell should make an effort to get closer to his own level.

Scared but more amused, Campbell knelt in front

of the boy, who reached out and touched the long
tendrils of Campbell's red hair from where it curled
out from under his tam. Then Campbell understood.
The Nez Percé had never seen a redhead before.
They were probably more in awe of him than he was
of them, which was going some, he figured. He
grinned at the boy, and pulled off his cap.

The Nez Percé gathered around, each wanting to
touch this blazing mane that reminded them of the
sunset. Campbell began to relax some, though it was
quite strange to have all these people chattering at him
in a language he could not understand in the least.

The Nez Percé began drifting away, until Campbell
was suddenly alone. With a shrug, he pulled the
mules and his horse off to the side and tied them to a
couple of small evergreen trees. He unsaddled the horse
and tended it. Then he unloaded the mules and took
care of them, too.

Just about the time he finished that, Finch and
Sharp came out of the lodges. They spotted him and
waved him over. He passed his friends' women, each
leading her man's horse, on the way.

"C'mon, boy," Finch said with a grin, "it's about
time ye met some of the *Nimipu*."

"The what?"

"The People. Well, actually, it means the Real
People. It's the Nay Percy name for themselves."

"Rather arrogant of them, isn't it?" Campbell
asked.

Finch laughed a little. "Damn near every one of
the tribes—everyone I've ary run across—has a name
means somethin' similar for themselves. The People
or the Real People or the Human Beings. I reckon there
is a certain amount of pride or arrogance in it."

Campbell nodded. He still thought it smacked of arrogance, but the Nez Percé he had seen so far certainly didn't come across that way.

Preparations for the feast were well underway as the three walked through the village. Finch and Sharp introduced Campbell to Stone Buffalo, Coyote Leggings, Hawk Strikes, and Talks of War.

Drums were beginning to beat, and the men drifted toward a large central fire. Elk and buffalo and mountain sheep were cooking over the fires. There was also dried salmon and camas bulbs.

Finch, Sharp, Campbell, Stone Buffalo, and Talks of War sat in a small group near the big fire. Many Bells served her man, Sharp; and Dancing Feather brought food to her husband, Finch, as well as to Campbell. After the men had eaten, Dancing Feather saw that Finch was filling his pipe. She hurried to get a burning stick from the fire to light it for him. As she did, she quietly brushed a hand across his bearded cheek, reaffirming her possession. He smiled at her.

Campbell was a little surprised when he saw that, but he said nothing. He just became more watchful. He noticed that Many Bells made similar small, loving gestures to Sharp. The Nez Percé warriors were the recipients of such things from their women, too.

Sharp's children, Spotted Calf and Otter, and Finch's son, White Hawk, joined the children of Stone Buffalo and Talks of War, playing around the fire, climbing over their parents and raising a nice little ruckus. Dancing started, but the small group stayed put, at least for now.

As Finch sat playing with his son and puffing on his pipe, he said, "We got us a little problem here."

The Indians—joined by Coyote Leggings now—

looked at Finch with interest, ready to help but reserving comment until they knew what help was needed.

"I got Dancin' Feather, and Ethan's got Many Bells," Finch said. "But young Alex here ain't got no one to keep him warm come the cold winter. Ye boys think we can find him a wife afore we pull out?"

The Nez Percé broke into grins, chattering among themselves while Campbell sat in red-faced embarrassment as Sharp translated for him.

Finally, with a serious face, Talks of War asked, "Is he a good man, my brother?"

"Well, now," Finch said slowly, "he's done all that's been asked of him on the trail and with nary a complaint. He's a strong ol' hoss, and there ain't no fear in him that this chil's been able to see. He's a good hunter and he's seems like the kind of man to take good care of a good wife."

"It is good," Talks of War said with a firm nod. "Your word is good. My daughter, She-Who-Is-Like-The-Morning-Sun, is of an age to take a husband. Many of the warriors, young and old, play the flute for her. There are many good men among them. But she will do well with your red-haired friend, I think."

"Well now, boy," Finch said, slapping Campbell on the back, "ye cain't go no better'n that. What do ye think?"

Campbell was still embarrassed, but he said calmly, "I'm nae sure, Caleb. What does she look like?"

They all laughed, both at Campbell's question and at his discomfort.

"Hell, boy," Finch said, "ye git up in them high mountains come winter, and the snow's a blowin' and the wind's a howlin', ye won't give a shit one way or t'other what she looks like. All's you'll care about is how much heat she'll generate."

"And come the huntin' seasons," Sharp added, "Ye maybe might worry about how well she works, if'n ye want the primest plews."

"And knowin' Talks of War, she'll be the hardest worker ye can find, boy," Finch tacked on.

Campbell shrugged. "If ye think it best, Caleb, I'll nae argue with ye."

It wasn't until the next day, though, that Campbell got to meet Morning Sun. Almost sixteen, Morning Sun was, in Campbell's eyes, a fine figure of a woman. A bit on the thin side, maybe, for his taste, but she was full-breasted and had fine, rounded hips. Her work-hardened hands were seamed and cracked, but that detracted from her beauty not a whit, as far as Campbell thought. She had clear, smooth skin on her face, and her eyes were bright and happy. Campbell enjoyed her quickness to laugh and the way she carried herself.

Sitting across the fire in Talks of War's lodge an hour after he had met Morning Sun, Campbell nodded. "Aye," he said, "she's a fine one, she is. I couldna do nae better. I hope I might be a proper husband for your daughter, Talks of War."

The Nez Percé nodded. "You'll do well, my friend." He liked Campbell already; thought him a decent, honest man.

"Go on to her now, boy," Finch growled good-naturedly. "She'll be waitin' for ye."

"Where?" Campbell asked, suddenly afraid.

"Ye saw that lodge bein' put up today?" When Campbell nodded, Finch said, "That be yourn."

"And Mornin' Sun's," Sharp added.

"There's no ceremony?" Campbell asked, rather befuddled.

"Nope," Finch said. "Now go on, boy. Your woman's waitin'."

"Aye." With a sense of excitement and impending doom, Campbell headed out. Morning Sun was, indeed, waiting for him. She had food prepared and a pot of coffee on the small fire. A bed of buffalo robes was laid neatly in the back, and other items in bags and boxes were stowed carefully around. A willow backrest awaited him. He sat tentatively.

Morning Sun served Campbell food and then sat nearby, attentive. Campbell ate the stew, hardly tasting it, not really wanting it but knowing that to reject it would be to reject her. "Do ye know who I am?" he finally asked.

Morning Sun stared at him, uncomprehending.

"Ah, sweet Jesus," Campbell muttered. Neither could understand a single word of the other's language. He touched his chest with a thumb. "Alex," he said. He repeated it several times. Then he pointed to her and said, "Morning Sun." He repeated that, too.

"Alex," Morning Sun said as she pointed at him. The word was mangled some, but understandable.

Campbell nodded and smiled. "Yes. Alex." He pointed to her. "And you?"

"Morning Sun." She smiled shyly, the action emphasizing her already prominent cheekbones.

"Yes," he said again. He smiled back, feeling a rush of warmth inside. He set down his horn bowl, and licked his suddenly dry lips. His eyes tried to catch hers, but she would not allow it. That angered him a little, but then he realized she must have a reason for it. He would have to check it out—tomorrow.

He could follow her glance toward the bed of robes behind him. "Yes?" he queried, his smile holding out hope.

"Yes," Morning Sun said firmly. She rose and held out a hand toward him.

Campbell took the hand and rose when she tugged a little. Seconds later, he was in a dream world, his naked, pale flesh pressed against her nude, dark skin. He had never even dreamt, really, of something so wondrous happening to him, and yet here he was, lying in the robes with a naked—and very willing—Indian woman.

In the next several hours, Campbell didn't think he would be able to get enough of this woman. She was exciting beyond his wildest imaginings. Once in a while, though, between times usually, he would lie there with the delightful She-Who-Is-Like-The-Morning-Sun in his arms and wonder if he was adequate enough for her. He always concluded that he was, since she was perfectly willing to come back for more.

It was still daylight when he fell asleep, he and Morning Sun entangled in each other's arms and legs.

10

They spent two more days in the village, but then it was time to leave. Finch was itchy to be on the move, considering that this was much later in the year than they were used to pulling out. If only he and Sharp had not had to take their friend east to catch the caravan. But there was nothing he or anyone else could do about that now, and he knew it.

Campbell was a little sad riding out of the village. In a few short days, he had come to like—and admire—the Nez Percé. Their ways were strange to him, but he accepted that, and even enjoyed some of the differences. In some ways, he longed to stay in the village, to set down some sort of roots.

Then he looked behind him, at the beautiful, clear-eyed woman riding the pale gray gelding behind him. Their time together in the village had been wonderful as they came to know each other a little bit.

Overcoming his initial hesitation, he had come to adore her, and was quite solicitous of her, much to Morning Sun's discomfort. She thought it was not right that a man should do so much for her. It was not the way of a Nez Percé man. She told him so, too—through Finch.

Morning Sun, in turn, had already become proud of her new man. It was so odd, she had thought several times, loving this pale-skinned giant. But he had shown himself to be worthy. She rode in silence, her eyes on the broad back and red hair of her man. Whenever he turned back to look at her, which he seemed to do with some frequency, she smiled at him, and felt a small thrill of pleasure when he returned it.

As he looked back at Morning Sun, the desire to be back in the village left him. As long as she was with him, things would be all right. He tried not to think of the oddness of falling in love so quickly with someone so foreign to him. He could not fathom it. Maybe he did not *want* to fathom it. He was worried that he might realize it was nothing more than infatuation because she was so different. Then where would he be, facing a whole winter cooped up in a small lodge in the mountains with a woman he could not stand. Or, worse yet, who couldn't stand him. Of course, he felt a jolt of excitement every time he looked at her. He figured it must be real.

The small group headed north and a little east. Two days after leaving the village, they slowed their pace considerably. Wherever they found beaver sign, they would stop and trap, spending as much time there as was reasonable. As soon as the take dropped off considerably, they would pull up stakes and move on out.

They worked their way slowly, methodically into and out of canyons and over passes, moving through the Sawtooth Range. Whenever they stopped to trap, they also took time to make meat. They would hunt whatever they could find and turn the meat over to the women, who in turn would make jerky or pemmican out of it.

Finch estimated it was around the first of September when they left the Nez Percé village, so they had little time to waste. Already the nights were cold, and they had seen snow squalls on several occasions. The longer they were out, the colder it got, and twice they had to sit out blowing snowstorms accompanied by a driving, moaning wind that whipped the snow into stinging little particles.

In a mountain meadow a month out of the village, they came across a party of five free trappers led by a man named Ed Warwick.

"Where're ye boys headin'?" Finch asked as they sat to meat and coffee.

"Had planned on winterin' up along the Flathead somewhere, but now we aim to spend it down near the Snake."

"What caused ye to change your mind, hoss?" Sharp asked.

"Fuckin' Blackfeet," Warwick growled. "Bug's Boys've been on the prod since we had that fandango with 'em down in Pierre's Hole after rendezvous last year."

"This chil' raised hair at them doin's," Finch said with a nod.

"Yeah, well, if'n you got yourself any thought of winterin' anywhere near Blackfoot country, best disabuse yourself of that notion, ol' boy," Warwick said flatly. He was not a man who scared easy, and he didn't like running, but he figured he and his four men—plus their women—were no match for an entire nation of angry Blackfeet.

"Well, this ol' coon wishes ye well, boys," Finch said evenly.

"You ain't aimin' to go up there, are you?" Warwick asked sourly, surprised. He was a little annoyed, too. If Finch, Sharp and their new partner undertook to trap in Blackfoot land, it would certainly make Warwick and his men look mighty fainthearted, if anyone learned of it, and someone was bound to. And once one man did, it'd be all over the mountains in no time. He scowled at the very thought.

"Mayhap," Finch said noncommittally. "I ain't thunk on it yet. I will say one thing, though: as much as I like raisin' hair on them fuckin' Blackfeet, I got no hankerin' to run into 'em."

Warwick and his men pulled out the next morning. Almost as soon as they were out of sight in the trees, Sharp asked, "Well, Caleb, are ye plannin' to winter up in Blackfoot country?"

Finch grinned lopsidedly. "And why not?" he countered.

"Because you'll get us all put under, you dumb bastard." He wasn't nearly as angry as the words.

"Ye scared?"

"Shit uphill," Sharp said almost good-naturedly. "Ain't no goddamn Blackfoot ary created by the Great Spirit can scare this ol' hoss. But give me one goddamn good reason why we'd want to risk our hair that way, what with them goddamn Blackfeet on the prowl."

"Jist because they are on the prowl," Finch said

simply. "I expect most of the other boys're gonna be like Ed and his critters—uneasy about winterin' up there. That means there's a heap of land up there ain't been trapped over. I aim to take advantage of that."

"You're more goddamn crazy than I thought," Sharp said with an easy laugh. "Gonna get us all rubbed out, sure as shit."

"Shit, ye lose your sense of adventure?"

"Hell, no, I ain't lost my sense of adventure. I got no hankerin' to lose my hair either." He grinned.

"Ye in or not?" The question didn't really need to be asked. There was no way that Ethan Sharp would pass up a challenge like this. Besides, they both knew all along where they'd be going; they were playing this out mostly for Campbell's benefit.

"Somebody's got to watch your ass," Sharp said with a grin.

"Then I best ask Alex." Finch looked at the Scotsman. "Well, boy, ye throwin' in with these two ol' critters?"

"Aye. I dunna know what to expect where'er 'tis we be goin', my friends, but I'm in with ye all the way."

They moved east through Lolo Pass, and then spent several days at the hot springs nearby. Campbell found the springs almost as good a tonic for his tired body as Morning Sun had promised him they would be. While he sat in one pool of steaming mineral waters, he thought how different things had become during the past two months on the trail. He and Morning Sun could now communicate pretty well. She was intelligent and quick to learn anything. He was surprised to find himself with something of a natural bent for learning languages, so he was picking up Nez Percé rather swiftly.

They pushed east soon after, moving through a crooked valley for several days before turning north. Campbell began to feel hemmed in by the tall, jagged mountains looming to both his left and right. He did not like the feeling, but he kept it to himself—in public. He did speak of it at night when he was alone with Morning Sun.

Despite his gloom, he found himself taking plenty of plews. They were thick and rich, the winter hair sleek and glossy. Campbell began to think he'd have no trouble at all making enough to outfit himself properly next year.

Snow fell regularly, and in spots the men had to walk out ahead of the animals, tramping down the snow enough so that the horses and mules could make their way through it without too much of a struggle. Fresh meat grew scarce, and the food they had was often iron-hard because of the frigid cold. The wind bellowed and roared through the saw-toothed peaks, whipping at them, sapping their strength.

At one point, in the midst of a raging snowstorm, Campbell fell flat on his face in the snow. "I dunna think we're goin' to make it, lads," he gasped. "Nae, we'll not make it." He managed to roll over, almost enjoying the sensation of the stinging snow on his face.

Sharp's temper was short. In a rage, he charged back to Campbell, grabbed him by the front of his heavy buffalo coat and jerked him to his feet. "Don't ye nary say such a fuckin' this to this ol' hoss," he snarled. "Ye aim to give up, we'll jist leave ye here to go under, boy. We ain't gonna set hyar and watch ye do it."

Resolve hardened Campbell's face, and he knocked

Sharp's hand off his coat. "I'll follow ye to hell an' back again, laddie, and ne'er lag in it. I'm just a wee bit tired is all."

"We all are, goddammit," Sharp said, not easing his harshness a bit. "But the animals ain't gonna last long unless we git 'em some fresh feed."

"Aye," Campbell acknowledged, ashamed of himself. "Then we best push on."

The storm's fury finally drained away and drifted off. The sun returned and soon they were tromping through slush. The next day, Finch rode out ahead and by early afternoon was back with his companions, urging them on toward the campsite he had found.

The mountain meadow was fairly large, and it was protected in large part by the gray stone edifice of the mountains on the west side. There were aspens in profusion, as well as pines of various sorts. Even a few cottonwoods reared up here and there. Game was not abundant, though there were signs of elk, deer, bear, buffalo, even moose. There was enough grass left to fatten the horses a little in the several days they spent there.

Then they pushed north again. It was into November now, and the threat of hard winter was never very far off. They saw plenty of snow, and even when the day was sunny, the sun did little to warm them or the earth. Eight days after leaving the mountain meadow camp, they could hear a great crashing roar ahead of them.

"What's that?" Campbell asked, riding up alongside Finch.

"I ain't sure, but it sounds like one big goddamn waterfall."

Finch proved to be right. They eased up on the

monstrous sound until they looked down at the billions of gallons of water pounding over the cliff.

"I ain't messin' with that, ol' hoss," Sharp commented.

"For once, I think you've got the right idea," Finch countered. He turned them east and north, working through a break in the jagged spires of several mountain ranges. A few days later, he turned them south into another valley. Once more the peaks rose tall, harsh, and forbidding on both sides of them, albeit at a little distance away. They came on the Middle Fork of the Flathead River, somewhere in the Flathead Range.

The next afternoon, Finch, who was in the lead, as he usually was, stopped. "This hyar's it, boys," he said with a firm nod.

The place did not seem all that impressive to Campbell. Not at first. Several streams entered the river within a short distance. And there were a number of beaver ponds around. That should make for some pretty good trapping, Campbell figured. As he took a closer look at the place, though, he realized its worth. There was plenty of wood. The trees and several cliffs kept out some of the wind, and probably would keep down the snow, at least a little. There was water, game, and even some forage for the animals.

The men set their traps and, in between trying to put up some emergency food for the animals, began building a rudimentary cabin.

"Ye ain't fixin' to stay in your lodge, Caleb?" Sharp asked, surprised. A tipi was a lot more comfortable than any cabin, and they had generally used them before.

"'Course I'm gonna stay in my lodge," Finch

retorted, as if Sharp had gone crazy. "But with the three of us now, we need us a place to store our plews and such, plus give the animals some protection."

Sharp nodded, relieved. While the women put up the lodges, the men set about cutting logs, making mortar out of mud, digging, and building. They still had to check their traps. In between times, they hunted as much as possible. That served two purposes—it added to their stockpile of meat, as well as their stock-pile of furs.

Deer and elk were plentiful, and there were still many bears roaming the region. The bear meat, rich with fat as the animals prepared for winter, was good for the humans. Beaver was eaten at times, and a fair number of deer and elk fell to the hunters' guns. They even fished once in a while, and late-flying geese were added to the larder.

Everything got done, though, and by the time the streams and ponds were too frozen over to allow trap-ping, the cabin was done. It was backed up against a cliff, using an overhang as part of the roof. It looked like hell, but it was big enough to hold all the horses and mules, plus it had plenty of storage room for pelts, equipment, and extra food. It would keep the animals warm and safe through the winter.

The humans, meanwhile, had their snug buffalo-hide tipis, which were warm with a fire inside, and could not be knocked down by the wind. They, too, would be safe and warm.

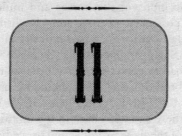

11

Winter hit hard, dumping plenty of snow. The ice grew thick; the wind ripped through the camp, battering the animals' shelter, trying to tear down the three lodges. The cold seemed to be attempting to freeze the peoples' blood in their veins.

For weeks on end the humans would venture forth from their lodges as little as possible. Being outside more than a few minutes brought a numbing, brittle, devastating cold to their bones that drove them back inside.

They all grumbled and bickered, but work—as well as friendship and mutual respect—kept them from all-out fighting with one another. And there was plenty to keep them busy. Skins had to be cared for sometimes, firewood and water had to be fetched. Broken gear and equipment had to be repaired. They hunted whenever they could; fresh meat was something of a delicacy now since it was so rare even to see game. The men got the horses and mules outside whenever possible to give the animals a little exercise.

One day after nearly two months in the camp, Finch and Sharp strapped on hastily made snowshoes. "Me'n Ethan're gonna take us a little journey, boy," Finch said to Campbell. "We should be back afore it gits dark. But if'n we cain't make it, we'll stay the night out there and head back in the mornin'. Ye take good care of the women and young'ns, ye hear?"

"Aye, I'll do that. But where're ye goin'?"

"None of your concern, boy," Finch said without rancor. "You'll know where we been when we git back. Don't ye fret none, though," he added. "Me'n Ethan ain't about to leave our wives and young'ns."

They slogged out into the frozen, snow-covered landscape, guns in hand, the locks wrapped in fur so they wouldn't freeze. Finch wore his buffalo coat, and Sharp his capote. Both had beaver skins wrapped around their faces, with slits cut for the eyes. They wore heavy mittens, plus thick boots of grizzly hide, fur inside and out.

They struggled back to the camp just before dark, faces pale from strain, cold and exhaustion. They entered Campbell's lodge, with Finch carrying the carcass of a mountain sheep across his shoulders, his knees wobbly from the weight of it. Sharp was right behind him, carrying both rifles.

Finch dumped the carcass on the ground and plopped down after it, too tired to even remove his bulky coat. Dancing Feather rushed in, saw him, and hurried to help him out of the coat.

The children came in next, and finally Many Bells, who went to help Sharp straight off. The women passed around food and coffee, the latter of which interested the two returnees a lot more right now.

"Did ye carry that thing back all by yoursel', Caleb?" Campbell asked.

"Naw," Finch said, breathing heavily. "Me'n Ethan took turns. Wasn't far. Maybe six, seven miles was all."

"But why did ye do it, mon? We have plenty of meat to last us."

"Wanted somethin' special," Finch said flatly. "This coon's plumb sick of jerky and pemmican." He knew he had been a fool, but he had been too itchy to sit in his lodge another moment. He had to get out and find something to do. The thought of some fresh mountain sheep was just enough to prod him.

"Besides," Finch added with a bright grin, "we nary did have us much of a Christmas celebration. I figured we was about overdue for a Christmas feast. Ain't that right, Ethan?"

"Yep." Sharp leaned over to light his pipe with the burning stick his wife held out for him. "Might's well git a little enjoyment out of life."

"You lads are crazy," Campbell said. "Nice crazy, I suppose, but crazy nonetheless."

Finch and Sharp laughed. "Mayhap we are," Finch said, "but this coon's gonna enjoy that sheep meat, goddammit."

The next day the sheep was butchered and the finest portion skewered on a green stick and set over the coals of the fire in Finch's lodge to roast.

From a sack, Finch produced a small batch of peppers, two sackfuls of beans, a few herbs, and a small pouch of cornmeal. From their own mysterious resources, the women came out with small piles of camas roots and wild onions. Everyone set about working, making small, flat corn cakes, cooking up the vegetables and beans with the herbs and peppers.

It was a rather festive occasion, seemingly made all the more so by the wind pounding on the skins of the lodge. The fire was bright and warm, the food delicious, and a jug of whiskey kept the men's spirits high. The men told tales and joined the women in the awl game for a while, circling their markers around a pegged-down deer skin, cheering or groaning over the four little sticks used like dice. Finally, they all stumbled to their own beds.

The months passed in slow boredom, a blending together of snowstorms, work, numbing cold, impatience, wind, irritation. Men and women both gaunted down and bickered a little. The children retained their vigor, since the adults made sure they had enough food to eat.

The horses and mules grew thin, getting less to eat each week. One of the horses finally had to be killed, and the people used the scrawny carcass for a little extra meat. They did the same to two more in the next month or so.

"Do ye think we'll make it through the winter?" Campbell asked at one point. He had seen severe winters back in Scotland. Indeed, the cold had been every bit as bad as it was here. Still, this seemed somehow so much worse. Probably, he finally decided, because back in Scotland he could face those winters in a strong stone house and with a much better supply of food.

"Sure," Finch said without hesitation. "Me'n Ethan've faced worse winters than this one." He considered launching into a tale, but the looks on everyone's faces squashed that idea.

They could sense a change coming along about the middle of March. It wasn't so much a break in the weather as it was a feeling. There seemed to be a change in the way the wind blew, combined with a slight lessening in the snowfall.

"Won't be long now, boy," Finch said to Campbell as they stood outside the lodges, their breath frosting in the air.

Finch's prediction was accurate, and within two weeks the daytime temperature rose above freezing for the first time in months. As the days dragged on, the snow began to melt; moss and grass began to pop up from under the snow.

"How long before we head out, Caleb?" Campbell asked one day.

"Another month at least. Late May or so, as best I can figure it. We need time to let the animals get their strength back. 'Sides, now's the best time for takin' plews, except for jist afore winter sets in."

Some weeks later, Finch looked up at the sky one morning and said, "We'll leave out in two days, Ethan. I reckon we can be ready by then."

"I reckon," Sharp grunted in agreement. "Where away ye want to head?"

"I don't like takin' the time, but I figure we ought to swing by the Nay Percy village and see if'n they can let us have some horses. We got a powerful lot of plews, but with them animals we lost over the winter . . . "

"Waugh, we sure are some short on horseflesh. I reckon the Nay Percy'll help us out some."

"Don't you always go to the village?" Campbell asked.

"Naw," Finch commented. "We usually jist meet 'em down at rendezvous. It's a far piece out of our way to go west to where the Nay Percy make their homes."

Campbell nodded. "Where is the rendezvous this year?" he asked, interested.

"Place called Ham's Fork. It runs into the Green River. There's been a couple there. It's a good place."

They pulled out on a morning that sparkled with bright sunshine. A few high clouds blew across the vast expanse of sky, but they held no threat of storm.

Once more they trapped as they rode, spending some days here, a few more there. They went south this time, through the valley before finally turning west, heading for Lolo Pass. Once beyond that, they turned southwestward, once again working through passes and canyons, across rivers and streams, around peaks and along valleys.

Twice they had to hole up to await the passage of a Blackfoot war party. The small group was seen neither time, much to their relief, but they stayed where they were for an extra day just to make sure the Blackfeet were well away from the area.

They finally spotted the village, and rode slowly in, accompanied by a phalanx of shrieking boys and young warriors. As they made their way past lodges, Finch said to Campbell, "Looks like we missed the big spring hunt." He pointed to the racks full of buffalo and elk meat drying in the sun.

Campbell nodded. He was a little disappointed, but not too much.

They paid their respects to Tall Clouds and then went to find places to set up their lodges. Eventually, they gathered in Finch's lodge, along with several of the Nez Percé men.

"Will you be staying long, my friend?" Stone Buffalo asked.

"Nope. It took us a heap of time to get here, and you folks've already been on the hunt."

"The hunt was a little early this year. The snows were gone quickly." Stone Buffalo paused. "What took you so long?"

Finch shrugged. "Pretty bad winter, for one thing. Plus we lost three horses over the winter. We had a good season, though, so we have many plews. Because we were short on animals, the ones we had were pretty heavily burdened. We didn't want to lose any more, so we took our time on the trail."

Stone Buffalo nodded. "You need more horses, then?"

"Yep."

"Then you shall have them." He grinned. "You wouldn't be in a hurry, though, just to get to rendezvous, would you?" he asked.

"Well, that might've occurred to me, yes." Finch laughed. "We're going to have a hard time making it there before it starts."

"We'll leave in two days?" Stone Buffalo said, making a question out of it.

"Suits this coon. How about ye boys?" He looked from Campbell to Sharp.

Both nodded agreement. Campbell was a little surprised that he had not needed Sharp to interpret for him. He had caught every single word. He knew he missed some of the nuances and such, but he had understood everything Stone Buffalo had said.

The rest of the day was spent in relaxing pursuits.

The three mountain men took full advantage, allowing their trail-cramped muscles to recover. They visited with friends, saw to their horses, ate and on occasion just lazed about.

The next day was given over to preparing to leave. The three whites moved through Stone Buffalo's vast horse herd and picked out several likely animals. Finch and Sharp also built a small fur press, and they baled the plews as best they could, generally in packs weighing ninety to a hundred pounds each.

They pulled out the next morning. There were perhaps seventy-five Nez Percé, all mounted: men, women, and children. Behind the women's ponies were travois that dragged their possessions. Young boys drove the horse herd, which was quite a sight, with nearly three hundred horses, almost all of them Appaloosas.

The mountain men and their families rode a little ahead of the main body of Indians, accompanied by several of their friends. Scouts ranged far ahead and on both flanks, keeping a watch out for enemies. This was the time of year when the Blackfoot, those Indians with wanderlust and warfare in their blood, were likely to arise.

They rode south for two days, until they reached the Snake River. Then they headed east, following roughly the Snake's wicked course. At times, they would have to ride miles away from the river to avoid an impossible canyon or peak. They took their time, burdened as they were by children and tons of food supplies and equipment.

They had been on the trail just over a week when two of the scouts came racing back to the main column. They spoke excitedly to Tall Clouds, who began issuing orders calmly but urgently.

Stone Buffalo trotted over to where Finch, Sharp and Campbell waited, wondering. "Blackfeet," Stone Buffalo said flatly, though there was a certain eagerness in his eyes.

"What's the plan?" Finch asked.

"There's a place half a mile ahead where we can defend the women and children," Stone Buffalo said. "We'll leave some of the men there to guard them. The rest of us will go out to meet the Blackfeet."

"How far ahead are they?" Sharp asked.

"Three miles. Maybe a little less. Almost right in our path."

"So then there's no avoiding them," Sharp said.

It was not really a question, but Stone Buffalo answered it anyway: "No. Is that so bad?"

Sharp grinned viciously. "Nope."

Stone Buffalo nodded and galloped off.

"You think the Blackfeet are here to fight?" Campbell asked. He was suddenly somewhat nervous.

"They didn't come all this way to pay their respects to us, boy," Finch growled.

12

"Take the women and young'ns and find yourself some cover back over in yon trees, boy," Finch said to Campbell. He pointed to the thin, long line of aspens and pines that edged up onto a slate-gray cliff.

"I'll do nae such thing," Campbell said, affronted.

"Don't get all het up, boy," Finch growled.

"Like hell, Caleb," Campbell snapped, his anger growing. "I'll nae have ye hint I'm a coward or somethin'."

"I ain't sayin' you're scared, boy."

"Then what is it? Ye think it's not me fight?"

"Now, I nary said such a thing, boy. It's jist that . . . "

"Well, by God, it's my fight as much as it is yours," Campbell said, having trouble controlling his anger. "If the Nez Percé are going to fight wi' the Blackfeet, then I figure to go into battle wi' them. The *Nimipu* have taken me in as one of their own, and I willna hide against responsibility."

"Well spoken," said Stone Buffalo, who had returned to stand unnoticed nearby. "Your words make my heart glad."

Campbell just nodded, still fuming.

"Now, listen to me for a goddamn minute," Finch said to Campbell, his voice harsh. "I ain't sayin' you're scared, and I ain't sayin' this ain't your fight. What I am sayin' is that me'n Ethan—who're a heap more accustomed to such doin's as fightin' the Blackfeet than ye are—need someone we can trust to watch over our women and young'ns. And ye got your own woman to tend to."

"And if that weren't enough responsibility for ye, hoss," Sharp put in, "we got us one hell of a heap of plews that we jist spent a winter freezin' our asses off to hunt. I ain't aimin' to see that Bug's Boys git their hands on 'em. We need ye to watch over them, too."

Campbell's anger fled, replaced by a spurt of pride that these men would entrust him with so much. He nodded. "Ye lads just take care of yoursel's," he said. "I can care for your women all by mysel' fore'er."

"Don't ye fret, boy," Finch said. "Now, go on, git them women and young'ns to safety."

Campbell nodded again and turned his horse. He began shouting orders in Nez Percé, glad that he was able to do so. Most of his commands were unneeded, though. The women and children knew what to do and had begun as soon as he had turned his horse.

As he herded the wives and children of the three mountain men toward the long string of trees and brush that lined the base of the cliff, Campbell noticed that all the other women and children also were moving swiftly in that direction. Old men, too, joined them. Campbell saw that four warriors accompanied Tall Clouds, ready to protect the old chief.

Campbell's small group got their horses and pack animals up near the cliff and tied them securely to trees. Campbell tied his horse with the others, took his rifle and then headed toward the edge of the trees, where he stood behind an aspen, rifle in hand and ready. The tree was not much protection, but he didn't think he would need any. He really could not foresee the Blackfeet breaking through the Nez Percé lines and reaching the trees here.

The three women got Finch's child and Sharp's two behind some brush up against the stone wall. Many Bells sat and Dancing Feather knelt around the other side of the brush, ready to help out where they could, or to protect their children if that became necessary.

Morning Sun went forward to be with Campbell. He was a little startled when she stopped alongside him and smiled at him.

"Go back wi' others," he ordered. "It's nae safe here, lass."

"I'll stay here and help," Morning Sun responded in English. She had picked up Campbell's language with almost as much ease as he had hers.

"No," Campbell said flatly. It was bad enough that he was responsible for the safety of Morning Sun, Many Bells, and Dancing Feather, plus the children and all the animals and furs. He didn't want to have to stand here worrying about Morning Sun.

"I can reload for you," Morning Sun said practically. "Dunna worry aboot me."

It was still mighty strange to Campbell to hear his

own brogue and rolling r's coming out of the lips of this beautiful young Nez Percé woman. He hesitated in responding, though. He didn't want her in any danger, it was true, but he was beginning to really think about it now. Would she be in any less danger back in the trees with the others than she was here? he wondered. It didn't seem likely, unless the Blackfeet overran the Nez Percé fighting force. If so, he could send her back, if he saw fit to. Though, at that point, he might need her help considerably. Then he finally remembered that Finch and Sharp had told him that Nez Percé women could be downright vicious when it came to fighting if they thought their families were in danger.

Still hesitant, Campbell looked around. The copse was crowded with Nez Percé women and children and ponies. There were not too many warriors of fighting age, but a few were scattered around. One was Coyote Leggings, who had taken up a position behind an aspen less than a dozen feet to Campbell's right. Standing beside him was his young wife, who had their infant child in a cradleboard resting against another tree.

Coyote Leggings smiled and waved.

Campbell returned the greeting, then said, "Have your woman take the child back with those of my friends. They'll be safe there."

Coyote Leggings hesitated only a moment, then nodded, turned and spoke to his wife. She picked up the child and hurried off.

"All right, Morning Sun," Campbell said, "you can stay with me—unless the Blackfeet get through to here." He pulled off his powder horn and shooting bag and handed them to her, hoping they would not be needed.

From where he was, Campbell could watch the slow-riding Nez Percé form a line across the open ground a couple hundred yards southeast of the cliff. From this distance, Finch and Sharp were easy to pick out—they were the only ones who had not stripped down to breechcloth and moccasins.

The last Campbell saw of them was when the Nez Percé suddenly bolted forward. He caught just a glimpse of the Blackfeet also charging. Then the two forces met with a crash, and within moments dust obscured most of the battle from Campbell's sight.

Campbell didn't like standing way back here, not being part of things, but he tried to control his itchiness. Only minutes after the battle began, though, he suddenly straightened. Five Blackfeet had broken through the cloud of dust out there and were racing toward him and the others.

"You ready, Coyote Leggings?" he asked, looking over at his companion.

The Nez Percé looked at him and grinned just a little, as if he were pleased with this occurrence. He nodded.

Campbell turned. "Go back to the others, Morning Sun," he said in Nez Percé.

"No." Morning Sun touched his arm lightly. "I'll be all right, as long as you're here."

He was about to argue, but the Blackfeet were approaching in a hurry. They seemed to be heading straight for him, but he didn't think that was any design on their part. It seemed that he and Coyote Leggings, with their women, children, and animals were the nearest.

He raised the rifle and braced himself against the thin aspen. He pulled the trigger, but the old flintlock misfired. "Och, shit," he muttered as he thrust the rifle at Morning Sun. "Hurry, lass."

Her movements were swift and sure, and in less than half a minute he had the rifle back in hand. He aimed again and tried once more. There was a small double flash and then a Blackfoot tumbled off his horse.

To his right, Coyote Leggings whooped and fired arrows, only one of which seemed to have any effect as another Blackfoot went down.

Campbell handed the rifle to Morning Sun again, and jerked out a pistol. He fired hastily and hit a horse. The animal fell in a tumbling pile, but the rider landed on his feet, stumbled ahead a few steps, then ran toward the copse only twenty yards away.

Campbell grabbed the rifle Morning Sun thrust at him and fired, but he was too quick and hit nothing. Then the Blackfeet were rushing into the trees. Campbell caught just a glimpse of Coyote Leggings leaping onto a Blackfoot pony behind the rider. Then Campbell had his hands full.

The Blackfoot who was on foot roared at Campbell. The Scotsman had only a moment to realize that the warrior was about his age and height, but outweighed him by thirty pounds or so. Then the Blackfoot was swinging a stone war club at his head.

Campbell jerked his rifle up crossways, in both hands. The war club hit the rifle, cracking the forestock, and knocking it out of Campbell's hand. Campbell fell back against the aspen, but bounced off and slammed a forearm into the Blackfoot's face. It seemed to have little effect on the warrior.

The Indian grabbed Campbell by the neck, lifted him and slammed him back against the aspen several times, rattling both Campbell and the tall, thin tree.

Suddenly Morning Sun hit the Blackfoot with his own war club. She was too short to really reach his head, though, and as a result, merely slammed him across the beefy shoulders.

The Blackfoot sort of growled. He pulled one hand from Campbell's neck and snapped the arm backward, hitting Morning Sun in the face with the elbow.

Morning Sun staggered away under the strength of the blow, and fell flat on her back. She lay as if dead.

It enraged Campbell. "Why ye son of a bitch," he roared. He stomped on the Blackfoot's right instep. It was enough to loosen the warrior's other hand on his neck a little. He broke the connection entirely by sweeping his right forearm across it.

Campbell smashed the heel of his left hand against the Blackfoot's cheekbone. The warrior was a big man, but Campbell was no lightweight himself, and the punch drove the Indian back a step. Campbell followed it up with two more blows to the face. Then he kicked the Indian in the leg.

The warrior seemed nonplussed by all this, and when his back hit up against another tree, he stopped and grinned a little. He spoke in his own language, which Campbell could not understand. Suddenly he leapt forward, meaty fist raised.

Campbell went to block the big arm and fist coming down at him from on high, ignoring the swift jab with the other hand with which the Blackfoot pounded into Campbell's ribs. "Och," Campbell wheezed.

The Blackfoot clubbed Campbell atop each shoulder with his fists, driving Campbell down to his knees. Campbell flopped back onto his behind. The

Blackfoot tried to kick him in the face, and he fell backward.

The warrior grinned again and pulled out a knife. He said something again in his own language.

Campbell couldn't understand the words, but he got the meaning, and he struggled to push himself up and pulled his own knife.

The Blackfoot knelt and began reaching for his hair, then suddenly fell on top of Campbell.

"Good Jesus," Campbell muttered, breathing hard with the Blackfoot's two-hundred forty pounds pressing on him. He wondered what had happened. He struggled and worked. It took a few moments before he was able to shove the Indian's body off of him enough to slip out the rest of the way. As he stood, Campbell saw two arrows in the Blackfoot's back. He figured they had come from Coyote Leggings.

When Campbell turned to thank the Nez Percé, he saw Coyote Leggings being knocked down by two Blackfeet. Campbell ran hard. One of the Blackfeet looked up, saw him coming, rose and turned to meet him, knife in one hand, war club in the other, a shield on his left forearm.

Campbell didn't slow down, unconcerned about the warrior's weapons. He just plowed into the warrior and drove him back until the Indian's back slammed against an aspen.

The warrior swiped at Campbell's head with the war club, but only caught his shoulder. Campbell jerked his head forward hard, cracking the Indian's nose with his forehead. With the Blackfoot momentarily dazed, Campbell yanked out his big butcher knife and shoved it deep into the Indian's belly. He pulled it free and rammed it home again twice more.

By then, the Indian was next to dead, and he sank to the ground.

Campbell whirled, ready to get the other Blackfoot who had been attacking Coyote Leggings, but the Nez Percé was just throwing the Blackfoot to the side. Both men scrambled to their feet.

Campbell started moving forward, figuring to grab the Blackfoot from behind, but Coyote Leggings shook his head. "This one's mine, my friend," he growled in Nez Percé.

Campbell nodded. As Coyote Leggings plunged his knife into the Blackfoot's heart, Campbell wiped his own knife off on his pants and put it away. Then he turned again. Morning Sun was still on the ground, looking dead. Campbell didn't think she could be dead. Or maybe he just didn't want to believe it could be true. He spotted Coyote Leggings's woman—Sees the Dawn—on the ground. She was bleeding, but she was moving.

He heard more yelling from farther up the line of trees and he snapped his head around. The last Blackfoot who had invaded the Nez Percé haven was racing along just outside of the trees, challenging any and all who were there. As the Blackfoot neared him, Campbell stepped out of the trees and stood.

The Indian jerked his horse to a stop.

"I'll have at ye, ye goddamn red devil, ye," Campbell announced. He pulled his tomahawk and stood there slapping the side of the blade against his left hand.

13

The Blackfoot smiled and dismounted. He had a stone war club in his right hand and a shield across his left forearm. He advanced toward Campbell, who also moved forward.

With every step, Campbell's anger increased. The possibility that Morning Sun was dead infuriated him, and he let that rage grow until he had a maniacal gleam in his eye.

The Blackfoot stopped and looked at him warily. Black Horse was not afraid of any man alive, but he was no longer sure this red-haired white man was really a man. Instead, he had the look of a black spirit about him.

Campbell never halted. He just pushed on until he was almost right in the Indian's face. Then he raised his tomahawk over his shoulder and brought it down hard.

Black Horse jerked his shield up to block the blow. He succeeded, but the blow had so much force behind it that the shield split, and the tomahawk still carried forward to break Black Horse's arm.

The Blackfoot grunted, but he was not about to give up. He swung his war club at Campbell's side, figuring he could easily smash several of Red Hair's ribs. Then the white man would be at his mercy.

But he only caught Campbell on the side with the handle of the war club. It hurt, but it did little damage. In fury, Campbell grabbed his tomahawk in both hands and began chopping at Black Horse, who futilely tried to injure Campbell with the war club.

Within moments, the Indian was down, but Campbell continued his assault. Until Coyote Leggings stopped him by grabbing his arm and talking quietly to him.

Reason slowly returned to Campbell, and he nodded. Then he turned and saw Morning Sun sitting up, holding her face in her hands. He rushed to her and helped her up. When she was standing, he realized he still had his bloody tomahawk in his hand. He wiped it off and slid it into his belt.

Morning Sun smiled at him, the blood from her nose making her face rather frightful. Campbell didn't care. He pulled her close. "Ye all right?" he asked.

"Yes," Morning Sun said. Her voice had taken on a sudden nasal sound. Campbell would have laughed at it if he didn't think it would hurt her feelings.

Minutes later, Coyote Leggings and Sees the Dawn joined them. Sees the Dawn had been clouted on the side of her head by one of the Blackfeet, but it had been a glancing blow, producing more blood than any real injury.

The four people turned as they heard whooping and shouting. The Nez Percé were riding back, seemingly victorious by the noise they were making. Sharp, Finch, Talks of War, and Stone Buffalo stopped by the small group.

"Looks like ye boys did all right for yourselves," Finch said, pointing at several of the Blackfoot corpses.

"Aye," Campbell said almost noncommittally. "And ye lads?"

"Whupped them fuckin' Bug's Boys good and goddamn proper," Finch crowed. "What ones we didn't put under, we sent packin'. Raised hair on three of 'em myself, but only scalped two. They picked up that other bastard afore I could take his hair, too. Ethan got him two, Stone Buffalo took the hair from four. Waugh! That's makin' 'em come now. Even the ol' fart over there"—he pointed to Talks of War—"got himself two."

Campbell's father-in-law didn't seem to mind being called an old fart. He grinned and showed off the two fresh scalps he carried.

"And the best part," Stone Buffalo said proudly, "is that we lost none of the People."

"Waugh!" Finch growled. "We are some now, boys, I tell ye."

"Ye took any hair yet, boys?" Sharp asked, looking from Campbell to Coyote Leggings.

"I did," Coyote Leggings said, holding up his trophies for all to see.

"Ye ain't done so, boy?" Finch asked, looking at Campbell.

"Ye mean ye want me to scalp these red devils?" he asked.

"Hell yes," Sharp said.

"I dunna know if I can do such a thing, mon," Campbell said.

"After what ye done to that one poor devil over there?" Finch countered. "Goddamn, boy, you're jist supposed to put 'em under and raise hair on 'em, not butcher 'em like buffler." He, Sharp and the Nez Percé all laughed.

Even Campbell grinned. It did not bother him to take a scalp. Or at least he didn't think it would. With all the butchering he had done, and having killed a few men before he had even come to these mountains, pulling the hair off a dead enemy shouldn't be all that hard. He just hadn't thought to do it yet. He had been more worried about Morning Sun.

With a shrug, he stepped off and soon was back with the scalps of the three Indians he had slain. "What do I do wi' these?" he asked.

"Tan 'em jist like ye would any other pelt," Finch said. "Ye can hang 'em from your war shirt, or your gun, or even your lodgepoles."

Campbell nodded.

They spent the night there, so they could hold a victory dance. Even Campbell joined in the dancing, stumbling over his own feet during the unaccustomed steps. He did not last long, though, since he did not like being seen to be so clumsy, so he sat with his friends again.

"Coyote Leggings's been tellin' us about what ye done today, boy," Finch said, impressed.

"Has he now?"

"Yep. Ye sure made 'em come now, or I wouldn't say so." There was no derision in Finch's voice.

Campbell flushed.

"Coyote Leggings says he's your friend for certain

now, boy. That ye saved his life and probably Sees the Dawn's, too," Finch said.

Campbell shrugged, still a little embarrassed. "Only after he saved my life. Aye. I came up against a Blackfoot that looked like one of yon mountains picked itself up and came a walkin' after me. Son of a bitch had me all ready to take me hair—or somethin' else—when the goddamn big fat lad falls on top of me, two of Coyote Leggings's arrows in his back."

"Waugh!" Sharp grunted. "That's some now. Seems like ol' Alex and ol' Coyote Leggings thar have got to likin' the each other more'n a bit."

"Hell, yes," Finch added. "Next thing ye know, they'll be settin' up a lodge together."

Campbell was angry at such talk, and he risked a glimpse at Coyote Leggings, who was laughing along with the others. Then Campbell realized that they might be joking with him, but there had been unmistakable pride and admiration in the two mountain men's words. His anger fled.

Campbell found himself accepted by the Nez Percé even more now that he had proved his mettle in battle. It was a little uncomfortable at first, but he soon grew used to it.

The entire group rode out the next morning, heading toward the rendezvous that was still a couple of weeks' travel away. They rode slowly, seeing no reason to rush. Finally, though, they began finding signs that the rendezvous wasn't too far.

The three mountain men stopped, and Sharp said, "I expect it ain't but a couple miles off. We best be gittin' ready."

"Gettin' ready?" Campbell asked.

"Yep. You'll see."

The three mountain men—plus their wives and children, along with Stone Buffalo, Coyote Leggings, and their families—pulled away from the band of Nez Percé. Finch led the others toward a muddy stream and found a pool that was relatively clean. Hobbling the horses, the men jumped into the pool and cleaned themselves up as best they could. When they came out to dry themselves in the sun, the women and children took their turn.

Campbell sat, somewhat self-conscious about his nakedness. He did enjoy watching Morning Sun, though. Still, he was sure he didn't like Sharp, Finch, Coyote Leggings, and Stone Buffalo being able to see her. There was nothing he could do about that, though, so he put it from his mind.

Soon they all began getting dressed. Campbell watched as Finch pulled on fringed buckskins of a golden autumn color and a long, heavily fringed war shirt. The shirt was loose fitting and had a circular design of colorful beads, glass, and shells on the front. "That's the fairest shirt I've e'er seen," Campbell said in admiration.

Finch nodded and sat to pull on moccasins. They had the same design as the shirt, only far smaller and in more muted colors. A tiny bell on the toe of each tinkled when he walked. His hat was a bear-fur cap with a hard-leather brim.

Sharp preferred a shirt of calico cloth in a rich green color, along with fringed buckskin pants that were bleached almost white. He pulled on heavy black boots and silver spurs with large rowels. He slapped a wide-brimmed felt hat on his head.

Realizing he was still naked, Campbell reached for his battered old buckskins, the ones he had been wearing since Morning Sun had made them for him soon after they had married. He pulled them on, unenthused. Standing against his two friends' finery, he looked mighty poor, and he knew it.

Coyote Leggings and Stone Buffalo were dressed in their best finery, too. The fringe on their shirts must've weighed twenty pounds all by itself, Campbell estimated. The bead work was stunning. Their leggings also were fringed and decorated, as were their moccasins. Each warrior wore a feathered bonnet.

Campbell sighed as he finished dressing. He sat again, feeling miserable.

The women and children began coming out from behind the brush, where they had dressed. Sees the Dawn and Traveler, Stone Buffalo's wife, were the first out. Their dresses were typical of their people, though somewhat more ornamented than usual.

Campbell shook his head when Many Bells came out, and soon after, Dancing Feather. They, too, had on typical Nez Percé dresses, but they were richer than the other women's, with more expensive beads in a larger quantity, plus bits of real silver. Campbell remembered now that his two mountain man friends had told him that as free trappers, they had to make sure their women looked the finest at rendezvous. Campbell vowed that he would see that Morning Sun was outfitted as well as any of the women at rendezvous, as soon as he traded in his plews.

Still, she looked a lot better than he did, with her dress about equal to those of Traveler and Sees the Dawn. The double yoke of her dress was heavily decorated and she had carefully brushed her hair, which hung down onto her shoulders in a raven cascade.

With a feeling of shame, he rose when Morning Sun came out from the brush. She looked shyly at him, hoping she looked good enough. When she saw him, her eyes got very large, and her mouth formed a small O. "I know," he said quietly, "I look like hell."

Morning Sun turned and fled toward the horses, leaving Campbell and the others standing there dumbfounded. She returned a minute later, looking abashed and carrying a parfleche. She handed him the hardened rawhide box. "I forgot," she said, shame reaching down into her innards.

Campbell looked at her, puzzled.

"Go," she said, pointing to the brush where the women had changed.

Still a little mystified, Campbell headed toward the brush. He set the box down and opened it, not believing what he saw. He hurriedly shucked his old clothes and donned the new ones that were in the box. The pants were the same as Sharp's and Finch's. The shirt was much like Finch's, though the pattern on the front was of lightning. The moccasins were soft and quite comfortable. There was even a cap—a wolf-fur version of his tam-o'-shanter. He slapped it on and stepped out from behind the brush.

"Well, look at this ol' chil'," Finch said in mock awe. "Goddamn, if he don't look somethin' like a real mountaineer."

"Close, I reckon," Sharp agreed.

"Go to hell, lads," Campbell said cheerily. His whole outlook had brightened considerably.

They all spent a little time decorating their horses with pieces of cloth, some daubs of paint, and bits of fur. Then they mounted up and rode out, heading for the rendezvous a couple miles away.

"There it is, boy," Finch said after a little while. He pointed to a camp that seemed to sprawl for a mile or more along a river.

They continued riding slowly, knowing that they would be spotted soon and that as soon as they were, they would have an audience for their entrance into the camp.

Finally they all stopped. "Ye ready, boy?" Finch asked, looking at Campbell.

"What do I have to do?"

"Ye jist foller us, boy." Finch looked at Sharp. "Ye ready, *amigo*?"

Sharp grunted and looked at his outfit one last time. "Let's go," he said.

"What about the women?" Campbell suddenly asked.

"They'll come along with the extra horses and the pack animals," Finch said. "Don't ye fret none about them. They been through this before."

Suddenly he bellowed and kicked his horse. Sharp, Stone Buffalo, and Coyote Leggings did the same, and then they were all racing away. A startled Campbell was only a few steps behind, his pony racing to catch up.

14

The five men thundered into the strung-out rendezvous camp, cheered on by trappers, traders, and Indians. Campbell brought up the rear, but not by much. The wild, screaming race had his blood surging and the pulse pounding in his forehead.

Campbell raced through the camp, seeing only a swirl of colors and hearing a blur of sound. He fired his rifle, as he had seen Finch and Sharp do, and he laughed. He felt wild, strong, free.

He pulled his puffing, blowing horse to a stop next to his four friends more than a mile through the camp from where they had started. He was breathing almost as heavily as his pony.

The five rode slowly back the way they had come, Finch and Sharp greeting old friends along the way. One of those they met grinned. "Ye make certain ye stop by my fire, Caleb, Ethan. We'll hoist a jug to the new season that's a comin'."

"I expect we can do such, ol' coon," Finch agreed.

"Who was that, Caleb?" Campbell asked as they continued their ride.

"Well, now, that was ol' Gabe Bridger himself," Sharp answered.

"I've heard of a Jim Bridger," Campbell said. "Are they related?"

"One and the same."

Campbell wanted to ask about the discrepancy, but Finch and Sharp were already talking with someone else.

They rode on, until they found their Nez Percé camp. Their women had already put up the lodges, started fires, and had food cooking. They were caring for the horses. The five men unloaded the pack animals, and then Sharp, Finch, and Campbell sat at a fire outside Sharp's lodge, plunking a jug of whiskey down nearby.

Other trappers began drifting by to tell of their news, and to hear the news from Finch and Sharp. They would spend a few minutes, have a bite of meat, a sip or two of whiskey, then drift on, looking for other old friends or for some activity.

Things quieted down after the first flurry of activity. Then Bridger suddenly appeared, sitting cross-legged next to Campbell at their fire. Campbell was startled, not having heard Bridger. The mountain man moved like Finch and Sharp did—silently.

"*Hola*, Gabe," Finch said, handing Bridger a jug.

"How's doin's, ol' hoss." He took a long swallow. "How's your women and young'ns?"

"Shinin'," Finch and Sharp echoed. "Yours?" Finch asked.

"Same. Who's your friend thar?" Bridger asked.

"This here's Alexander Campbell," Finch said. "Fresh over hyar from Scotland."

"Well, not exactly fresh from Scotland," Campbell said quietly.

"That's true," Sharp said. "He's spent a winter up in the Flathead Mountains with me'n Caleb."

"Do tell." Bridger reached out with an open hand. "How's doin's, ol' hoss?" he said. "Come out hyar to make your fortune, did ye?"

"Aye," Campbell said, nervously shaking Bridger's hand. He had heard this man's name numerous times since he had left Saint Louis. He was something of a legend.

"That shines, boy," Bridger said with a grin. "Plumb shines. Jist as long as ye don't take my share of it."

"I dunna want anyone else's fortune," Campbell said with a grin. "Just my own." He paused, then went ahead. "I was wonderin', Mister Bridger, why your name is Jim but the lads call ye Gabe?"

Bridger scowled, then grinned. "An ol' hoss named Jed Smith hung that on me. He was a pious goddamn critter and said I was as glum as the Angel Gabriel. It's kind of stuck since."

"Me'n Ethan found ol' Alex a wanderin' alone beyond South Pass," Finch said to break the suddenly uncomfortable silence that had arisen. "Goddamn, but he was a green son of a bitch." He laughed. "The chil's learnin' fast, though. Goddamn if he didn't raise hair on three fuckin' Blackfeet a couple weeks ago on the way here."

Bridger pounded Campbell on the back. "Lord a'mighty that's some, boy," he said with renewed exuberance.

Campbell winced a little at the pounding. Bridger

was a brutally strong man, he thought. But he grinned manfully. "I dinna have much choice," he said.

"Don't matter why's the reason, boy. Anytime one of us ol' beavers can raise hair one of Bug's Boys is shinin' doin's."

Finch and Sharp agreed heartily.

"How's about one of you boys pass that jug back over this way," Bridger said. "I've got me a powerful thirst."

Finch hefted it and found it almost empty. He handed it to Bridger and then called for Dancing Feather to bring another. When she did, he pulled the cork and drank deeply before passing it to Sharp.

The jug made the rounds as Bridger began yarning. The tall, bull-necked mountain man, crinkle-faced from the weather, stopped occasionally to swallow a healthy dose of whiskey.

Finch and Sharp had heard all the stories before, but they didn't mind hearing them again. Bridger was about the best tale-teller in all the Rocky Mountains. He had been in the mountains more than a decade now and had seen probably more country than any man alive, so he had a plethora of tales to tell. Most, though, had at least a kernel of truth in them somewhere.

Finally Bridger stood, weaving some from the effects of the whiskey. "Well, it's been plumb plea-surable talkin' with ye boys, but this chil's got other things to get to. I aim to clean ye all out at gamblin' afore ye leave, so's I'm expectin' to see ye again." He stumbled off into the darkness.

Sharp slumped to the ground, almost in the fire, the whiskey having gotten the better of him.

"Think we ought to move Ethan away from the fire a wee bit before he gets himsel' cooked?" Campbell asked Finch.

"I reckon."

The two stood, their movements loose and sloppy. Staggering, they dragged Sharp away from the fire and managed—somehow—to get him into his lodge. Then they stumbled off to their own lodges.

None of them was all that much the worse for wear the next day, at least after several cups of coffee and some fresh buffalo meat. They took it easy through the morning, but then in the afternoon, they headed for adventure in the rendezvous.

Campbell was rather in awe. There was so much activity that it almost reminded him of Philadelphia. They walked past lodges and tents, small knots of men gambling and shooting. They passed trade blankets and shooting contests. They saw half a dozen brawls and more than a few men staggering around drunk.

There were men with a variety of accents—French, Spanish, Scottish, Irish, German, and a few Campbell could not place.

Then there were the Indian villages: Shoshones; Crows, led by the half-black mountain man Jim Beckwourth; Flatheads; Bannacks; other bands of Nez Percé; even some Utes. The men were impressive for the most part, dressed in their finery, with their long, black hair flying, as they strutted around the camp.

It was their horsemanship that really impressed him, though. He had seen how well the Nez Percé rode, but that did not prepare him for the exhibitions he saw. Every now and again, a group of Indians would ride along and show off for the white men, wheeling and turning their horses in intricate patterns.

The best of the Indian riders were the Crows. At one point, one Crow warrior came racing past, one hand through a knotted loop in the pony's mane, one leg slung over the horse's back. While thundering along, he fired three quick arrows, which thudded closely together into a small target. Still at full gallop, the Crow pulled himself upright and war whooped. He was followed by three others, all of whom did as well as the first.

"I've seen it," Campbell said afterward, "but I still canna believe it."

"Them Crows can really ride," Finch said. "Like they was born on a horse. I ain't on the friendliest of terms with the Crows, but I admire 'em for their horsemanship."

By early evening, they were back at their own camp. Campbell ate at his own lodge, but then went to Finch's. Sharp was there, and the two had already broken out a jug. To be polite, Campbell had a few sips from the jug. He left soon after, accompanied by a fair amount of derision from his two friends, heading for his robes. Morning Sun had given him a hard time for having gotten drunk last night; he wasn't about to face the same thing again. Especially after she had been so angry at him when he had kidded her because her face was still so mottled with bruises from the fight with the Blackfeet. Alexander Campbell was no fool.

In the morning, Campbell figured his two friends would be under the weather, so he strolled off by himself, taking a look around. No one seemed to think he was out of place, and he relaxed. By midmorning, though, he was missing Morning Sun, so he went back to the lodge, where they made love for a while. When he came back outside, he spotted Sharp and Finch down by the creek. He waited for them.

"Ye two look like ye've died and canna figure out

ye should fall down," Campbell said almost gleefully when Sharp and Finch staggered up.

"Ain't none of your goddamn concern, boy," Finch growled.

"Jist let us be for a time, hoss," Sharp added. "We'll be all right after a spell."

By midafternoon, when Campbell next saw them, the two seemed to be doing a lot better. They found Campbell wandering around, looking, listening, learning. "Ye look some better," Campbell said. "I dinna think ye'd make it."

Finch laughed. "We've recovered, but we decided this mornin', we might be a mite ol' for such doin's."

"Too often," Sharp tacked on. "This chil' ain't all that ol'."

"You're older'n Christ," Finch snapped, but he laughed again. He looked at Campbell. "Ye join in any of the contests, boy?"

"Nae. I was not sure they'd let me."

"Hell, boy, anybody can take part. Long's ye got somethin' to put up for a wager."

"I have nothing to use for such. Not until I trade my plews in."

"Should've said somethin'," Finch said. "We could've let ye have a little advance."

Campbell shrugged. He did not like being in debt, and had no plans to start now. Not when he had a fair catch of beaver, plus a number of other pelts just waiting to be traded in for cash money.

"Looks like they're about ready to start them a foot race. Why don't ye join in? Me'n Ethan'll wager on ye. With them long legs of yourn, ye ought to do well."

Campbell looked dubious, but then he grinned. "I

was thought to be fast when I was back in Scotland," he said. "Aye, I'll do it."

The races had already begun, with just a few men running at a time. Other men, red and white, stood and cheered or made catcalls. The three friends muscled their way through the small crowd nearby so they could watch a race or two. Finch and Sharp made a few small bets, coming out about even.

Then a big, broad-chested Crow stepped up to the starting line. He was alone, since no one seemed willing to challenge him.

Bridger moved out and bellowed, "Who hyar'll challenge Eagle Foot?" When no one moved, he said, "Come on now, boys, surely there's one chil' out there thinks he can beat this hyar Crow." He looked around, searching faces. Of the ones that were sober, none looked interested. Most of the men knew of Eagle Foot, and knew the Crow had never been beaten.

"Here's your chance, boy," Finch said to Campbell. "Ye think you're fast, ye take up that Indian's challenge. Ain't nobody ary beat him."

"Nae, Caleb. It's be foolish to take such a challenge."

"Christ, boy, whar's your sense of adventuresomeness?" Finch demanded.

Campbell shrugged. "How far's the race, lad?"

"Couple mile, I expect. Ain't nobody measured it out."

"I dunna think I want to risk it," Campbell said doubtfully.

"Hell, boy, what've ye got to lose? Jist wager a couple plews against whatever he puts up. Then ye cain't git hurt too much even if that critter does whup ye."

Campbell stared at the long-legged Indian while

his two friends goaded him, and Bridger exhorted the crowd. Then he heard Bridger say, "I'll wager my Hawken gun that nobody hyar can beat that chil'."

"How much we expected to put up agin ye?" someone in the crowd yelled.

"Jist two plews is all," Bridger said.

Campbell suddenly stepped forward. "I'll take your wager, Mister Bridger."

The crowd roared, and bets were quickly placed. Finch looked at Sharp. "Think we ought to back that ol' chil'?" Finch asked.

"Waugh!" Sharp spat. "He's our friend, ain't he?"

"I was afraid ye were gonna say that."

They went around, betting plews, a little cash, some trade goods.

Campbell stood next to the Indian at the starting line. The Crow stood with his arms across his big, bare chest, grinning. He had no fear that he would lose this race.

Finch and Sharp strolled up to Campbell. "Ye best win this hyar race, boy," Finch said in mock fierceness. "We bet a heap on ye."

"I dunna think ye should've done that, lads."

Finch grinned. "We got faith in ye boy."

Campbell nodded, uncomfortable. He undid his belt and handed it with his pistols, knife, and tomahawk to Finch. Then he pulled his shirt off. With so much riding on this race, he wanted every advantage he could get. Since Eagle Foot was wearing only moccasins, breechcloth, and leggings, Campbell figured he should get down to pants and moccasins.

15

The crowd quieted, and Bridger said, "When I fire my pistol, ye boys take off. Then run down yonder through the camp to that post, around it and over toward the east. There's another post set up in the Shoshone camp over thar, then ye head back hyar, on this hyar side. Ye got it?"

Campbell and Eagle Foot nodded.

"All right, riddy," Bridger said. He held his pistol high and then pulled the trigger. The noise also triggered a roar from the crowd as the two racers bolted. The spectators cheered and whistled and then moved across the camp, hoping for a vantage point when the contestants headed east, wanting to follow the race as closely as possible.

Campbell felt good running. He could feel the long muscles in his thighs stretching and tightening, as he flowed into an easy, long stride. He glanced at

Eagle Foot. The Crow was running easily, big chest not straining. Campbell brought his eyes forward, spotting the first post. He intended to be a step ahead of Eagle Foot when he got there and rounded it. Ten yards from the post, he put on a little burst of speed and moved a few steps ahead of Eagle Foot. He tightly rounded the post, with the Crow right on his heels.

Campbell slowed his pace back down again, wanting to save his strength. The Crow matched him stride for stride, seemingly without exertion. The blood pounded in Campbell's ears, and his eyes narrowed to slits to block out the wind.

He tried for another burst of speed when he neared the other post, but Eagle Foot knew his plan now and paced him, then edged him out at the turn. The Crow took the lead by a few steps when Campbell made a wider turn than he wanted.

Campbell shook his head in anger at having been beaten out at the post, but he set his mind to the task ahead.

The two men raced through the Shoshone camp, pounding along. Campbell caught up to Eagle Foot and ran right alongside him. A stitch crept into Campbell's side, and he began sucking for air a little. As they roared past the edge of the main trapper's camp, Campbell whispered to himself, "Come on now, lad, ye can do it."

Campbell let out a bellow and exploded, pushing himself as hard as he could. He could feel his legs beginning to cramp, but he ignored it as he ran and struggled to breathe.

Eagle Foot was surprised, and he struggled valiantly to catch up, but Campbell had him now. Campbell sprinted for all he was worth, arms and legs pumping furiously. With every step, he put the Crow just a fraction farther behind. He passed the finish line and stumbled to a halt. He bent over, hands on knees, as he sucked desperately for air.

Men gathered around him, whooping and shouting. Finch and Sharp shoved their way through the crowd and pounded happily on Campbell's back. "Ye were some now, boy, I tell ye," Finch said.

"Quit your beatin' on me, lads," Campbell wheezed. "I canna take it."

"Sorry, boy," Finch said, not feeling bad about it at all.

Campbell straightened, still gasping. Bridger walked up, looking a little rueful. He had his .50-caliber flintlock Hawken rifle in hand. He held it out. "Hyar ye are, boy," he said a little sadly. "It's a good rifle and shoots plumb center. It's kept this ol' chil' alive more'n once."

Campbell took the rifle and held it almost reverently. He looked at its sleek lines, the dark wood of the stock, the short, heavy, octagonal barrel. Still looking at the rifle, he said, "I'll take good care of it, Mister Bridger. Aye." Then he glanced up and saw the sadness on Bridger's face. He hesitated only a moment then held out the rifle, saying, "I canna take your rifle from ye, Mister Bridger. It would nae be right. Take it back, and ye can give me a fair exchange of plews instead."

Bridger looked indignant. "I ain't ary gone back on no wager that I lost in all my days, goddammit, and I ain't about to start no such goddamn doin's now."

"But . . ."

A broad grin suddenly cracked the seams of Bridger's face. He started laughing, a deep, booming sound that started way down inside and roared up and out. "Goddamn, boy, ye won that rifle fair and square, and I ain't regrettin' for a minute losin' it. Not after seein' a race like that'n. I misdoubt I'll ary see another so good agin, so's it were worth it."

"Are ye sure?"

"Why certain I am, hoss. I can git me another rifle. And after that race ye run, ye deserve it." He slapped Campbell on the shoulder. "Jist use it well, boy. And mayhap you'll kill one of them goddamn Blackfeet with it of a time. Besides, I saw that piece of shit ye was carryin'," he said of Campbell's rifle, which Finch had fixed with dried rawhide after it was broken in the fight with the Blackfeet. "It's time ye had a proper rifle." He walked away, still chuckling.

"Well, boy," Finch said, "ol' Gabe were right. That was some goddamn race. I nary knowed ye had it in ye."

Campbell glanced at him with wide eyes. "And ye bet all ye had on me despite that?" he asked.

"Hell, no," Finch said with a laugh. "We got us some winnin's on ye, but we nary bet all we had. We jist told ye that so's you'd run your best."

"Ye sons of bitches," Campbell growled.

"It worked, didn't it, hoss?" Sharp countered, laughing also.

The humor of it suddenly got through to Campbell, and he joined his friends' laughter. "I'll tell ye, though," he said, "there were a few times durin' that race when I dinna think I could win it. That Eagle Foot sure can run."

"He can for sure," Finch said. "Ye hungry, boy?"

"After that, I sure am." He cradled the Hawken in his left arm as they headed back to their camp.

Along the way, they came on Bridger again.

"Some of the boys're fixin' to have a fandango over at my lodge tonight. Why don't ye come join us?"

The three agreed.

Just after dark, they headed for the doin's. Men were kicking up their heels to the sounds of a scratchy fiddle and a worn harmonica. Others stood in a ragged circle, clapping, stomping, and hooting, more or less in time with the music. Most had a jug or large tin cup in hand. Finch and his two companions filled their mugs from the open barrel of raw whiskey.

The three watched for a while, sipping whiskey and joining in the noisemaking. Finally Finch said, "C'mon, Ethan, let's get in on these doin's." He pulled a yellow calico handkerchief from the pouch at his belt and tied it around his left arm. Then, as the music began again, he and Sharp began dancing with each other, swirling and stomping on the hard-packed earth around the great bonfire.

"What's the handkerchief for, Mister Bridger?" Campbell asked.

"Call me Jim. Or Gabe, if you're of a mind. That handkerchief signifies that for the purpose of this dance hyar, Caleb's takin' the woman's role. Since there ain't no real women about, some of the men got to act the part whilst they're fandangoin'. It don't really mean nothin' more'n that, and most of the boys take their turn at it."

Campbell nodded. "But what about Indian women?" he asked. "There's a many of them hereabouts, I've seen."

"Indian women can't do no real dancin', boy," Bridger said, as if he thought Campbell was an idiot for even suggesting such a thing.

"Anybody ye know of here have some bagpipes?" Campbell asked.

Bridger thought about it for a few moments, then nodded. "A feller named MacGregor over at the American Fur Company's tradin' tent's got one, I think. Why?"

"Think the boys'd like some bagpipe music for somethin' of a change?"

Bridger laughed. "These critters're always lookin' for somethin' different."

Campbell nodded. "Where's this tradin' tent?" he asked.

Bridger gave him directions, and Campbell trotted off. He returned twenty minutes later with a large sack.

"What's in the sack, boy?" Finch asked.

"Ye'll see in a moment." He went near the fire and opened the sack. As he pulled out the large black-and-plaid set of bagpipes, a red plaid item fell out.

"What'n hell's that?" one man asked.

"Bagpipes," he said, a little confused. Certainly all of these men had seen—and heard—bagpipes before.

"I know that, ya dumb shit, ya. I meant that." He pointed to the item that had fallen.

"'Tis a kilt," Campbell said tightly after picking the item up and looking at it a moment.

The man, somewhat drunk, walked over and snatched it out of his hands. "Looks like a goddamn dress to me, boy," he said. He spun around, holding the kilt in the air. "Lookee hyar. I think we got us a woman on our hands." He laughed nastily, but the other men were silent.

Campbell's face grew hard. He had had no intention of wearing the kilt; hadn't even known it was in the sack with the bagpipes. Still, he didn't think these men needed to hear that. "I dunna think you're very funny, laddie," he said in controlled tones. "Now, if ye dunna mind, I'd like the kilt back." He held out his hand, glaring at the man.

"Aw, the little girlie wants his dress back. Ye fixin' to put it on to entertain us boys?"

"I have nae argument wi' ye, laddie. Now ye've had your little joke and your laugh. I'd appreciate ye givin' it back here." His voice was still even, but his anger was rising.

"I figure I'll jist give it to one of my squaws. Less'n ya want to come take it from me?" The last was a challenge.

Campbell's eyes were cold and hard. He set the bagpipes carefully down. "I dunna think ye want to challenge me, laddie."

"Ya don't, huh?" The man—Abel Daniels—looked around the fire. "By God, boys, I think I've jist been challenged."

The other men were stone-faced. Daniels was known throughout the mountains as a bully and a coward, except when he thought he had the upper hand. Or when he was drunk, which was often the case. With few exceptions, Daniels had no friends in this crowd.

The unkindly faces did not deter him. He grinned viciously and spat tobacco juice on the ground. He dropped the kilt in the dirt and then, without warning, lunged at the young man, tackling him.

Campbell fell, grunting when his hip hit on a stone, but he rained punches on Daniels's head and back. The two rolled over and over in the dusty earth, right through the fire, and almost over the bagpipes, each gouging and punching, mostly ineffectively.

Finally they fell apart and struggled to their feet. Daniels was panting.

Daniels lunged again, but Campbell sidestepped. As Daniels rumbled past, Campbell hit him on the back of the neck with his fists locked together. Daniels went sprawling in the dirt.

Daniels stood, weaving a little, his eyes piggish with hate. He closed in, hoping to get Campbell in the circle of his brawny arms. But Campbell snapped punches at his face. Daniels grunted as each landed. Then a mighty right hand from Campbell caught Daniels in the forehead and Daniels fell backward, landing with a thud.

He was a little slower getting up this time, but he finally did. He spat again, dribbling brown juice over his chin. He angrily wiped it off with the back of a hand, then pulled his knife. He moved cautiously toward Campbell, who uneasily pulled his own knife. Campbell had not wanted the fight to go this far, but he was not about to back down now.

The crowd, which had been shouting and goading on the combatants, grew hushed. This had suddenly turned into serious business. The men in the crowd remained mostly silent, watching intently as Campbell and Daniels feinted and parried.

Daniels made one move and his blade sliced across Campbell's left forearm. The Scotsman ignored it.

Confident now, Daniels pressed forward, heartened by Campbell's steady retreat. Suddenly Campbell stopped and in one quick spurt, reached out and grabbed Daniels's knife arm. Surprised, Daniels tried to grab Campbell's knife arm, but he missed, and Campbell's blade sank deep into his guts.

Face to face with the fetid mountain man, Campbell

jerked his knife upward, tearing through muscle and organs until being stopped by the ribs or breastbone.

Daniels stumbled backward, and Campbell pulled his knife free. Daniels dropped his own blade and looked at the ragged, gaping hole in his stomach. Intestines had spilled out. He looked up at Campbell in pain and wonder. He sank to his knees and then pitched forward onto his face.

Campbell wiped his blade clean on Daniels's shirt and then slid the weapon into the scabbard. He shook his head in annoyance that it had come to this. Suddenly a cup of whiskey was thrust under his nose. He took it, nodding thanks to Finch, and drank the whiskey all in one long gulp. He looked at Finch.

"Don't fret none, boy," Finch said. "Men like Daniels're fools. Jist like everybody else here, he's seen a kilt afore. Don't nobody know why he chose to make somethin' of it this time. But he was jist askin' to have someone jam a butcher knife in his meatbag."

Campbell nodded and turned. Daniels's body was gone, and the men were preparing to resume their fandango.

Sharp handed Campbell the kilt, brushed off and folded neatly. "Where the hell'd ye git this, hoss?" he asked.

Campbell shrugged. "I dunna know where it came from. I traded a couple plews for the bagpipes. I figure the kilt was in the sack with the pipes."

"Goddamn fool," Finch muttered. "Daniels, I mean. Makin' trouble and gettin' his foul ass rubbed out over somethin' Alex didn't even know about."

"Some men jist wasn't born with any sense," Sharp noted.

"Well," Finch said, "now that those doin's're over,

what say ye break out them bagpipes, boy, and play us a tune or two?"

Campbell hesitated only a moment, then nodded. He puffed up the big plaid bag, and then started playing. The wheezing, infectious drone sounded almost odd in the cool mountain air.

An old, red-bearded Scotsman who had been trapping since well before Campbell was born stopped in front of Campbell. "Your playin' reminds me of the highlands, laddie," he said wistfully. Then he turned and jammed his hands on his hips. He kicked up his right leg so his heel passed his right knee. He dropped the foot and did the same maneuver with the other. He twirled and spun in a spirited Scottish reel, smiling in joy.

"Hell, I can do that," Finch said. He moved up alongside the old man and tried to follow his movements, stumbling and then nearly falling a few times. Then he began to get the feel and rhythm of it and moved more smoothly.

Finally the song wheezed to an end. Finch stopped and turned. "Well, c'mon, boy, play us another."

16

Daniels's property was sold off the next morning at a lively, argument-laden auction. Campbell bid on and won one of Daniels's horses; Sharp settled for a horse and a jug of whiskey; and Finch came away with the dead man's knife and tomahawk.

Old Gabe Bridger, though, got Daniels's rifle, a .54-caliber Dickert. "Now that's a shinin' rifle, boy," he gleefully told Campbell.

"I'll trade ye so ye can have your own rifle back," Campbell said seriously.

"Naw, boy, ye keep it. This'n'll do me jist fine."

It was over quickly, the dead Daniels having little in the way of worldly possessions. Then the men went back to their spree.

The days passed all too quickly for Campbell, who was in an almost constant state of wonder. He joined in some of the contests, finding his shooting adequate in general, but sorely lacking when tested against most of the other mountain men. He enjoyed it anyway.

Campbell traded in his plews, with Sharp and Finch watching over him to make sure he didn't get taken any more than the rest of them. He made sure he got himself enough supplies for the new season. With the cash left over, he bought Morning Sun a wide range of foofaraw. He also gambled with some of it, on horse races, foot races, the hand game and more. He had learned early on that the mountain men and traders would bet on anything and everything. He willingly joined in. He lost more than he won, but he didn't much care. It was all a good time.

At one point, he bet about all he had left on Finch's Appaloosa in a race. He came away a winner that time, with a pile of plews, several extra knives and twenty dollars' worth of trade goods.

There were frequent brawls, what with all the arguments over gambling, women, and just plain stubbornness accentuated by whiskey. Rarely did the brawls turn lethal, but there was plenty of bloodshed nonetheless.

Rendezvous was a rollicking, feisty, hell-raising time, and Campbell enjoyed it thoroughly. But it had to come to an end sometime, and two weeks after their arrival, Campbell, Finch, Sharp, their women and children, and the Nez Percé began preparing to leave.

It was decided that the three mountain men and their families would head west and a little north with Tall Clouds's Nez Percé, spend a few days there, and then head north for their trapping.

They took a few days getting ready to go, making

sure they had the supplies they would need plus enough horses and mules to carry them all, as well as some extra horses just in case.

Campbell had outfitted Morning Sun with all sorts of geegaws and foofaraw, and just before they were ready to pull out, he realized he had no cash left. He complained about it to his two friends.

"Well, what the hell were ye expectin', boy?" Finch asked with a snort. "You're a free trapper, by God, and ye and your woman should shine."

"But I thought . . ."

"Jesus, hoss," Sharp snapped, "if you're gonna fuss and carp like this all the time, me'n Caleb'll leave ye hyar at rendezvous and ye can make your own way into the mountains."

"Now, I dinna say I wanted such a thing, Ethan," Campbell said half angrily, half soothingly. "I just thought I'd have a little more to show for a winter in the mountains."

"Ye got plenty to show for it, hoss," Sharp said, a little mollified. "Ye've had yourself some shinin' doin's hyar. Ye got ye a shinin' woman." He grinned. "Ye got good *amigos*."

"Aye," Campbell said seriously, "I canna deny that. Any of that. Still, I had been hopin' to have enough money to send to the Fraziers—for the horse of theirs I sold, and for all the help they gave me."

"From what ye told me, boy, it sounds like they did such out of the goodness of their hearts. They won't expect ye to pay 'em back."

"I suppose ye're right, Caleb," Campbell said reflectively. He sighed. There was nothing he could do about it now, but he couldn't help wishing it were different.

They pulled out the next day, the men and women still dressed in their finery. The day after, though, out came their plainer, working outfits.

The large group moved slowly, not feeling pressured. It was only the middle of July, and there was no need to rush. There was plenty of time for the Nez Percé to make some raids on the Blackfeet and still easily make the fall hunt. For the trappers, it would be a couple more months yet before the beaver fur was thick enough to be worth taking.

So they moseyed along, taking their time, hunting fresh meat whenever possible, which was most days. It provided a varied diet for the travelers, with buffalo, elk, deer, and antelope being taken with regularity.

It took a month for the group to make it to the Nez Percé homeland. The trappers spent a week there, then they pushed on, heading west along the Boise River. They turned north and followed the Salmon River, trapping its tributaries, inching their way ahead. It was into September, and the air was cool during the days, and cold at night. They got some snow flurries now and again, but not too much yet. The plews they took these days were good, but not really winter prime. Still, they'd bring a good price down at rendezvous the next year.

As September turned into October, and the autumn deepened, they curled west along the Snake River, still trapping, making camp for a few days at each place and then moving on. They also traded when they could, with Flatheads and Bannacks, Salishes, Spokanes, and Palouses.

By mid-October, they reached the Columbia River, and turned north along it, until two weeks later they came to the Spokane River. They turned east, trapping and trading their way along that river for several weeks.

Along about the first of December, as best as Sharp could figure it, they were camped on the eastern reaches of the Spokane River. Winter was pressing on them, and they were getting snowed on regularly. They were also taking prime winter plews.

"Where away ye want to go now, Caleb?" Sharp asked one night in that camp.

"North?" Finch suggested.

"To where?"

"Canada."

"What in hell ye want to go to British land for?" Sharp asked, a little annoyed.

Then Finch grinned. "Damn, it ain't bad enough you're afraid of the goddamn Blackfeet, you're also afraid of the British. It's a sorry thing for this ol' coon to know."

Sharp raised up onto one ass cheek and let loose a loud, wet fart. He settled back down. "That's about all I got to say about that buffler shit."

Finch laughed. "Well put," he said dryly. He thought for a while, and then nodded. "East, and maybe a little north. Follow the Coeur d'Alene up into the Bitterroots on this side of the Divide. There's plenty of beaver streams up there, and some valleys where we ought to be able to find some shelter for the winter."

"I reckon that shines with this hoss," Sharp said after a moment's thought.

"What about ye, Alex?" Finch asked.

The Scotsman shrugged. "I dunna any of these places," he said. "If ye lads think they'll be good for trappin', I'm all for it."

"It's mighty close to Blackfoot country," Finch warned.

"I'm not afraid of the Blackfeet," Campbell said with bravado.

"Ye should be," Finch said seriously.

"Aye. Let me say it again. I'm afraid of them because they're mighty warriors. That much we've seen. But I'm nae going to let that put me off from trappin' in their lands if that's where the beaver be."

Finch nodded.

They moved out the next day, pushing a little harder, but it still took them two weeks or so to find a place that Finch thought would suffice for wintering. They built a cabin, as they had done the year before, for the horses and plews and storage. They set their lodges up amid the trees, and were settled by Christmas, for which they had a small feast of moose and elk.

Settled in, they made their last push for plews before winter closed down on them. Finch suggested that they split up, each taking a different area.

"I ain't sure that's such a good idea, Caleb," Sharp said.

"Don't be such an ol' lady, Ethan," Finch said soothingly. "There ain't nothin' to fear out here. The only Indians that're close by are the Coeur d'Alenes and the Pend d'Oreille, and they ain't nary hurt no one."

"I thought ye said we were close to Blackfoot country," Campbell interjected.

"Yep," Finch said with a shrug. "But them red devils're on the other side of the Bitterroots, and they're gittin' ready for winter. They ain't gonna be botherin' nobody."

Sharp didn't feel good about it, but he acquiesced.

They worked that way for a week, then two, then

three. Then one day Finch heard a shot off in the distance to the east, where he knew Campbell was supposed to be working. "Shit," he grumbled. He grabbed his rifle and ran, crashing through the underbrush, heedless of the noise he was making. He reached the spot where he figured Campbell would be and stopped. Panting, his breath frosting in front of his face, he looked around. There was no sign of the Scotsman.

Sharp suddenly burst out of the trees a few feet away. "Whar's Alex?" he asked.

Finch shrugged. "Jist got hyar. Ye heard a shot?"

"Yep. Thought I heard some war whoops, too. It's what brought me runnin'."

"Fuckin' Blackfeet," Finch said flatly.

"I reckon. Ain't no other Indians out here gonna cause that kind of trouble. Ye said so yourself," Sharp added sourly.

Finch ignored the intended insult. He began searching the banks of the creek. Sharp watched him a moment, then waded through the icy water to the other side and started looking around. Suddenly, Sharp shouted, "Caleb, over here!"

When Finch had splashed across the rushing stream, he stopped and knelt alongside Sharp, who pointed to the ground. "Fuckin' Blackfeet all right," Finch grumbled.

"Them boys's headed east and mighty goddamn fast."

Sharp nodded. He stood and pushed along the bank, eyes searching. He stopped again, then called, "I found blood."

Finch hurried over and looked at the dark splotches on the snow and a rock. "Think it's Alex's?" he asked.

"Hell if I know. Ain't no one I know of can tell the difference between Blackfoot blood and white man's blood." He sighed and leaned on his rifle. "There ain't much, though. If'n he's hurt, he cain't be too bad off."

Finch nodded. "I figure there ain't but five, maybe six of 'em."

"About what I thought. Ye aim on chasin' after 'em?"

"Hell, yes. If they got Alex, I want to get him back afore those red devils start sportin' with him. Besides, they cain't be more'n a few minutes ahead of us. We move now, we'll likely cut their trail afore long."

"What about the women and young'ns?"

"We're gonna have to leave 'em here, I reckon. The idea don't shine with this ol' coon, but there ain't much else we can do. They'd hinder us too much on the ride, and they'd only be in danger when we run them bastards to ground."

"What about the Blackfeet?" Sharp countered. "If one war party's around, there might be others."

"Might be, but I doubt it. They've counted coup and I expect they're on their way home. I suspect those red devils was returnin' from a raid on the Flatheads or somethin' and come on Alex out here by himself. They took advantage."

"Ye nary thought they'd be by here this time of year, but they showed up anyway, didn't they?" Sharp was annoyed.

"It's too late to do anything about that now," Finch growled. "But we cain't take the women with us. The young'ns'd be even worse to tote along. At least here they can fort up if the Blackfeet come back. They can defend themselves some if they're cornered."

"I reckon you're right, hoss, but this ol' beaver don't like it none." He spat into the snow. "Well, shit, if we're gonna go, we'd best move our asses. Them Blackfeet ain't dawdlin'."

Finch nodded, and the two men ran toward their lodges. While Sharp began saddling their horses, Finch explained to the women what had happened. Then Finch joined Sharp. By the time the horses were saddled, the women had packed two sacks of food— enough to last a few days—plus powder and ball.

"Figure we ought to take some trade goods?" Sharp asked.

"What'n hell for?" Finch countered.

"We catch them Blackfeet, maybe we can make a trade for Alex."

"Ain't likely with those fuckin' red devils."

"True, but ye nary can tell when such things'll come in handy with some other Indians if we need some supplies or something."

Finch shrugged. "Can't hurt, I suppose."

"Many Bells," Sharp called. When she popped out of the lodge, he said, "Git us some trade goods and load 'em on a mule. That big, brown one, I suppose. He's the fastest and strongest."

Dancing Feather came out of her lodge, looking worried. "Now ye listen to me, woman," Finch said. "Ye and the others stay close to the lodges. Mayhap you should all move into one so's you'll be close. Ye got plenty of meat made, and there's a heap of fire-wood. Ye can melt snow for water instead of goin' down to the creek. I don't want ye takin' no chances. I don't figure the Blackfeet'll be back, but ye nary can tell what those red devils'll do. They do show up, ye all git to the cabin. Ye got our extra rifles and such."

Dancing Feather nodded and Finch touched her cheek. "And ye watch over Mornin' Sun, ye hear?"

An inconsolable Morning Sun had remained in her lodge, as she had since shortly after she found out that Campbell was missing.

Dancing Feather nodded again and hugged her man once.

Many Bells came up towing a pack horse. She handed the rope to her husband.

"Ready, ol' coon?" Finch asked.

"Let's do 'er."

They rode out fast. Finch looked back once and noticed that the women were already preparing to make prayers to the Great Spirit to guide them on their journey and to make strong medicine to protect the two men.

17

Campbell had just tossed a dead beaver onto the riverbank and was resetting the trap when he heard something that didn't seem right to him. He couldn't quite put his finger on it, but there was something wrong. He waded out of the cold creek and grabbed his rifle, which was lying right on the bank. Almost instinctively, he checked it over. It was loaded and primed. He crouched and looked around, trying to grasp whatever it was that had alerted him.

Suddenly a Blackfoot popped into view from behind a rock. The Indian's face was painted a sickly yellow speckled with red. Then he disappeared.

Campbell crouched there, still trying to determine whether he had really seen an Indian or if he had simply imagined it.

Then four of them were charging at him, appearing as if by magic from behind rocks, trees and brush. They came silently and fast.

Campbell brought the rifle up and fired hastily. One of the Blackfeet grunted with pain and fell. He was up in a moment, though, clutching a bloody arm, but staying where he was.

Campbell jerked out his pistol, but the warriors were swarming around him now. He tried to fire, but one Blackfoot hit him across the chest with his lance. The gun discharged, the ball hitting the mud of the riverbank, as Campbell staggered backward from the blow. He fell into the water.

Campbell lurched back up, knife in hand. A smack on the head from the lance made him reel. He made two ineffectual swipes with his blade before the three Blackfeet—plus still another one who had materialized—pinned his arms. His hands were swiftly tied behind his back with horsehair rope.

One of the warriors yipped out a victory call, before he was silenced by the angry eyes of another, who appeared to be the leader of the group. Black paint covered his entire face, except his eyes, which were encircled with white paint.

Another rope was looped around Campbell's neck, and he was dragged into the brush, where a sixth Blackfoot held horses. Moments later, he was thrown onto a pony, his feet tied under its belly. The warriors mounted and they all rode hastily away.

They rode through the night and all the next day, stopping only briefly every once in a while to gobble down a little pemmican and give the horses a rest. Campbell had noticed that the warrior he had shot was bleeding, and he hoped the blood would leave a trail in the covering of snow. But on their first stop, the other Blackfeet poulticed and bandaged the man's arm. Campbell's hopes of leaving a trail for Finch and

Sharp to follow dimmed considerably, though he figured the trail would be clear enough unless they got more snow.

They finally made a small camp, and the Indians ate deer meat they had taken during the ride. When they were sated, they pitched some scraps of food to Campbell. Though they were rank and covered with dirt, Campbell downed them. It was the first food he had had since the last meal he ate at his camp. It tasted terrible, but wasn't much worse that what he had had on the ship, he figured. He knew it would help him keep his strength up, at least a little.

After eating, Campbell looked over the Indians. They were a rough-looking lot. Two were almost handsome under the hideous paint. One was a gross-featured man with nothing but cruelty in his eyes. They were bundled up in blankets and mittens, with buffalo wool caps. They looked warm. They also looked determined. None had said a word to him through the long ride.

"Do any of ye speak English?" he asked. "Or Nez Percé?"

The black-faced one, whom Campbell figured was the leader, looked at him impassively. "I speak the white-eyes' talk—some," he finally said. His voice was deep, resonant, angry; his accent thick.

"What's your name?"

"I'm the Wolf Who Speaks to the Sky," the Blackfoot said with obvious pride.

"What do you plan to do wi' me, Talking Wolf?" Campbell asked.

"What you think?"

"Kill me—after torturin' me some."

Talking Wolf said something to his companions,

and the Blackfeet laughed and spoke amongst themselves for a few moments.

"I dunna think it's very funny," Campbell said stiffly.

"We're not gonna kill you," Talking Wolf said.

"Then what are ye to do wi' me?"

"We'll take you to our village," Talking Wolf said. "There you'll be kept as a . . ."

Campbell's eyes widened. He had heard of white men captured by Indians and being turned into virtual slaves. That was what he thought Talking Wolf was trying to say but could not because of the limitations of his command of English. That made him shudder a little. He knew—or had heard—that such unfortunates were regularly beaten, constantly abused and poorly fed, if fed at all. Still, it would mean he would be kept alive, and as long as he was alive, he could always hope for escape. He had no intention of being a slave in a Blackfoot village.

But there could be no attempts at escape now. Not tied hand and foot, surrounded by a war party of Blackfeet. He could, however, dream of the day it would happen. He must, he knew, do what he could to stay alive—and healthy. Then keep his eyes open for an opportunity to escape.

The Blackfeet continued their fast ride the next morning, heading east. Eight more days of hard, almost nonstop riding through mountains brought them to a village along the Milk River in the foothills between the mountains and the plains.

When they rode into the village, Campbell was spit on by men and women alike. Women rushed forward to hit him with sticks and pelt him with stones. Little boys did so, too, racing recklessly forward to count coup on the white prisoner's legs, which were still tied under the pony.

Remembering what Finch and Sharp had taught him, Campbell hardened his face, keeping his eyes impassive. He stared straight ahead, hoping the Indians would see him as impervious to pain and insult and then maybe he could earn their respect. That would make escape that much easier.

The warriors eventually stopped the abuse, for the time being. Campbell was not at all sure, though, that it had anything to do with a burgeoning respect for him.

He was taken to a greasy, patched tipi that had seen too many years of wear. An old man, wrinkled and creased with age, his hair white, stepped out of the lodge and stopped. Two women, seemingly even more ancient than the man, followed him outside.

Talking Wolf dismounted and went to the old man. "Father," he said in Blackfoot, "your women are old and have trouble with their many tasks. That is not right. A man who has brought so much glory to the People should not suffer such indignities."

The crowd was gathered behind Campbell, listening intently. The Scotsman had no idea what Talking Wolf was saying to the old man, though he guessed it concerned him in some way.

"So I, the Wolf Who Speaks to the Sky, give you this white-eyes. He will help you and do what your women can't. He will bring you food, and carry wood for your fires. He will bring up water from the river, and make sure your fire never goes out. He will do all that you order."

The old man nodded solemnly. He walked haltingly to Campbell and looked up at the tall white man on the horse. He grinned, showing almost toothless gums. "It is good," he said.

Talking Wolf puffed out his chest in pride. He walked to Campbell and looked up at him. "You go with Rides Far now. You do what he says or you'll face me. I'll be watching you." With a wave of the hand, Talking Wolf indicated that another warrior should untie Campbell and see that he was given over to Rides Far.

When he dismounted, Campbell's knees almost gave way. He had hardly eaten in the past four days, since the war party had suddenly turned stingy with meat, and he had hardly been off the horse since he had been captured. He had to hold on to the pony to keep from falling.

The two old women tittered while inspecting his teeth and his red hair. They tugged at his clothes and poked and prodded him with greasy, gnarled fingers. Campbell stood unwavering, allowing their inspection, staring straight ahead.

Finally, the two women quit their jabbering and nudging. They went inside the lodge. Talking Wolf shoved Campbell from behind, directing him toward the tipi. With rubbery legs, Campbell moved ahead. Inside, one of the women pointed to a pot hanging from an iron tripod over the fire. She said something in Blackfoot.

Campbell didn't understand her, but he hoped she was telling him to eat. He knelt by the fire and picked up a horn bowl. He scooped some of the odorous stew into the bowl and began eating. The few pieces of elk meat in the stew were rancid, and the stew itself was filled with fat and gristle. But Campbell ate it and then took some more. He knew he had to keep his strength up if he was to escape.

He was allowed to sleep then, which he did gratefully, even though the blanket he was given was filthy and rank. It was not very warm either, and somewhere in the night he rose and moved closer to the fire.

Campbell's work began in the morning. He carried firewood as the two old women walked behind him, prodding him with sticks. He brought buckets of water and did other women's work. Almost every move he made was accompanied by a running stream of Blackfoot words, which he assumed were insults. He could not be sure, because he could not understand them.

He cared for the old man's few horses and was made to wait on the three old people. The family's biggest need was food, and so Campbell was given an old bow and two arrows. He was allowed to hunt, but only with the boys, and always under the watchful eyes of some of the warriors. Talking Wolf seemed to enjoy this duty, and would insult him regularly.

Campbell swallowed the insults—once he began to understand them—and the demanding tasks, but his humiliation was great, and he never stopped thinking of ways to escape. He knew it was foolish yet, though. He was too well guarded, and it was winter.

He hunted as well as he could, which was not very well at all since he did not know how to use a bow and he only had the two arrows. Still, he worked hard at trying to get better with the weapon, knowing that the more food the old family had, the better he would be fed.

Winter in the Blackfoot village was hard. It was bitter cold all the time, and it seemed to snow every other day. He was given an old knife, one with a dull blade, to chop through the ice on the river so he could bring water to the lodge, and he often had to find his way around the village with water or firewood in raging snowstorms. The old people, cooped up inside most of the time, became irritable and would often scold and beat him, lashing out at his legs with willow saplings.

His clothes soon became tattered and worn through in spots, but there was no buckskin for him to make others. His moccasins wore through, and his feet nearly froze every time he went outside. He had no coat, since the Blackfeet had taken his buffalo coat—which had been lying on the riverbank while he worked his traps—right from the start.

Making everything worse were his thoughts of Morning Sun. He missed her something terrible, and every time he saw one of the young women from the Blackfoot village walking around, he would be reminded of Morning Sun. He missed her quiet, inquisitive ways, her comforts and her infectious giggle.

Campbell's facility for languages stood him in good stead, though. Within a few weeks, he understood many simple words. Within a month, he was able to speak to his captors and understand what they said to him.

As the winter deepened, he went to Rides Far one day and asked, in Blackfoot, "May I have a small piece of fur to make new moccasins with?"

The old man picked up a piece of firewood and hit Campbell on the side with it. "You have done nothing to deserve new moccasins. My wives have no new moccasins. I have no new moccasins. You won't have any either."

The blow with the stick had not hurt, but it was annoying. He almost always addressed the Blackfeet in their own language these days, but now he said, "Dumb bastard."

The old man, not knowing English, still knew he had been insulted. "You shouldn't speak to me that way," he said. "It isn't right."

Campbell choked back his anger and smiled. In a pleasant voice he said, "Go to hell, ye old skunk-humper."

Seeing the smile, Rides Far also smiled. "That's better," he said.

Campbell continued to hunt when he could, and now he could go alone, though on foot. The Blackfeet knew he would not get far in the snow and cold, so they were not worried about him running. He also was improving a little with the bow, and had more success these days.

One day he shot an old buffalo bull he found floundering in the deep snow. He sliced off a hunk of skin where the fur was thickest. Quickly he stripped off his shirt and wrapped the bloody skin around his chest before putting his shirt back on. He had been out for more than two hours and had been chilled to the bone, but the still-warm skin served to heat him a little.

He ate some of the liver raw, and then butchered out as much meat as he thought he could manage, which he wrapped in another piece of the hide. Tying some rawhide ropes around the bundle, he towed the meat-filled skin across the snow as if it were a sled.

Rides Far and his two wives were pleased with the meat, as stringy as it was, and allowed Campbell to sleep near the fire that night instead of next to the flap, as usual. As the old people went to sleep, Campbell peeled the buffalo hide off his chest, the dried blood having made it stick. He fashioned a rude pair of moccasins out of it and put them on, luxuriating in their warmth.

Campbell worked harder now, seemingly trying to please Rides Far and the two old women. It paid off for him. He was beaten less often and they even had a kind word for him on occasion. Rides Far even began speaking of the possibility of actually adopting Campbell, of having the Scotsman become a Blackfoot. "Would you like that?" Rides Far asked one night.

Campbell smiled and spoke in English. "I'd rather eat the ass of a week-dead buffalo."

"It is good," Rides Far said in Blackfoot, beaming.

18

Word of Rides Far's plan, if that's what it could be called, quickly reached the ears of Talking Wolf, and the warrior began to follow Campbell everywhere, taunting him, goading him, trying to make the white man fight. He wanted to kill him, but to do so cold-bloodedly would insult Rides Far, and Talking Wolf did not want to do that. But if he could push Campbell into a fight, he could kill him without guilt. He could probably even manage to make it look like he was saving Rides Far's honor in the doing.

Campbell knew what the Blackfoot was trying to do, though, and would not fall for it. He swallowed the insults and abuse with an icy smile fixed firmly on his lips. "I'm nae goin' to let ye do it, Talking Wolf," he said one bitter cold afternoon while he was out gathering wood. "Ye canna force me into it."

"You'll never become one of the People," Talking Wolf vowed.

"You going to stop it?" Campbell asked, trying to keep the haughtiness out of his voice.

"Yes," Talking Wolf hissed.

"Why're you doing this to me?" Campbell asked, trying to remain calm. "If you hate me so much, why didn't you kill me right off?"

Talking Wolf gazed down at Campbell from his height on his pony, looking grim. "I wanted you to suffer. To be humiliated. To pay for what you've done."

"What've I done?" Campbell was baffled.

"You're the Red Hair, killer of my son, Black Horse."

"Who?"

"My son, Black Horse."

"I dunna . . ."

"You're the Red Hair, who killed Black Horse when we fought the Nez Percé during the summer moons."

"I was nae the only one to kill Blackfeet that day," the young mountain man said defensively. "Many Blackfoot died then. And Nez Percé, too." He knew the last was a lie, but he thought it might calm Talking Wolf some.

"I watched as you killed my son," Talking Wolf said in flat, harsh tones.

"He was trying to kill me." Campbell still didn't know which Blackfoot Talking Wolf meant, but he felt justified in having killed all three that day.

"You chopped him to pieces," Talking Wolf said with a catch in his throat. "You made it so his spirit will wander forever. For that you must pay!"

Campbell now knew which of the warriors Talking Wolf meant, though it didn't change his situation all that much as far as he could see. "He would've done the same to me if he had the chance."

Talking Wolf didn't want to hear it.

"You looked for me all that time since?" Campbell

asked. That was worrisome. Such an obsession on Talking Wolf's part could make his situation now even worse.

"Yes." The word was ugly, would have been even if it had been in English. "You and your friends were hard to track, but I finally found you."

"How'd you know it was me who did it?"

"There are many white-eyes who as big as you are," Talking Wolf said, regaining his composure. "But there are not so many your size and have such red hair. That made it easy to know who you were."

Campbell nodded. With that knowledge, he realized just how bad his situation was. He had thought that perhaps if Rides Far got his way and Campbell was adopted into the People, it would be easier to get away, since he would be trusted then. Now he knew, though, that Talking Wolf would never permit such a thing. He also knew that he would have to get out of this village and soon. Talking Wolf would see him dead and butchered if Rides Far pressed with his plan.

Talking Wolf jerked his pony's head around and rode off. The look in his eyes let Campbell know that he faced even worse treatment than he had received so far.

Over the next several nights, Campbell killed Talking Wolf dozens of times in his dreams, but he did nothing. He kept a cold calmness in his demeanor, seeming to have accepted his lot, though he seethed inside. He did think seriously about escaping. He knew he no longer had much time. He had been waiting, he realized, hoping that Finch and Sharp might come for him, but now he knew that would not happen. They either figured he was gone under, or they were dead themselves. He would have to do it himself.

He had to make plans, though, and gather what

supplies he could. He managed to hide a few rabbit skins and some scraps of old buffalo hide. With them and some sinew, he made himself a sort of cape to try to keep off the worst of the cold. Then he would not have to use his thin blanket as a wrap when he went hunting.

He wore the miserable cape without pride, suffering the jeers of the warriors as they strode about in their buffalo robes or heavy blanket coats.

Talking Wolf saw the cape and saw another chance to taunt the Scotsman. He rode his pony over and poked Campbell with the tip of his lance. "I like your little robe," he said. "I think it will look good on my sister. Yes. I'll take it."

"Eat shit, ye red devil," Campbell said calmly, though there was fire in his eye.

Talking Wolf's eyes narrowed, and he drew the lance back, as if ready to run Campbell through.

"Do your worst, lad," Campbell said. "Ye dunna scare me."

Talking Wolf relaxed a little. "You speak bravely, white-eyes," he said in Blackfoot. "Not wisely, but bravely." He started to circle the horse slowly around Campbell, who did not move.

A powerful blow to the back of the shoulders sent Campbell to his knees. The shaft of the lance bent and almost broke as it smashed against Campbell's back.

Campbell fell forward and rested on his hands and knees. He sucked hard to try to ease the pain, and he gritted his teeth, determined not to give into it. Finally he pushed himself to his feet. He looked at the Blackfoot with fury on his face, but he forced it to blankness a moment later.

"Yes," Talking Wolf said arrogantly, "it will look good on my sister."

"Then I'll make her a present of it," Campbell said gallantly. He stripped off the thin cape and held it out. Talking Wolf moved his lance out so that Campbell could hang the cape on the end. As he was about to do so, Campbell pulled it back just a bit and dropped it. Then he turned and walked back to the firewood he had been collecting.

As he walked, he hunched his shoulders, expecting to feel the sharp bite of the lance at any moment. But it never came. An enraged Talking Wolf scooped the cloth up with the point of his lance and trotted off. Campbell breathed a sigh of relief and went back to work, hoping it would keep him warm.

Over the next few days, Campbell increased his preparations for escaping. He became quite adept at pilfering small pieces of meat and hiding them under the ice so the dogs would not find them. He also squirreled away small pieces of fur, and he stole a blanket one night when it was left lying outside. He hid that, too.

A cold, starry night came, one with little wind for a change. The temperature hovered near freezing—almost warm after the past two months. It was now or never, he thought. As soon as the old ones were asleep, Campbell arose and took a buckskin sack. He took tinder and a burning-glass and stuck them in the sack. He also took one of the old women's butcher knives and stuck it in his belt. He squatted by the fire, warming himself, and finished off the kettle of stew and the pot of coffee. Finally he grabbed a large stick he could use for firewood. Then he wrapped his blanket around his shoulders and slipped out of the tipi, casting a wary eye about.

He scooted around the lodge and dug up his stash of food and other small supplies and stuffed them into his sack. He stood. Hearing something behind him, he turned.

Two feet away stood Talking Wolf, grinning evilly. Without a word, and without hesitation, Campbell cracked the Blackfoot on the head with the tree limb. Talking Wolf fell.

Campbell hesitated only a moment. He wanted nothing more in the world right now than to kill this Indian. Then he decided against it. It would take too much time, and would increase the chances that he would be seen. Instead, he ran for the horse herd. He picked a likely looking mount and hopped on. As he raced out of the village, he looked back. Talking Wolf was on his feet and shouting. The village burst into activity.

Within moments, ten Blackfoot warriors were mounted up and chasing him. Campbell did not spare his horse. The cold bit through his thin blanket and clothes and made breathing hard. He put his head down and urged the horse to go faster.

Campbell looked back and saw that the Blackfeet were gaining on him as he sped along the snow-covered ground. One warrior outpaced the rest. He nocked an arrow and let it fly.

The arrow sliced across Campbell's left leg before piercing the pony's side. The horse's front legs buckled, and Campbell was flung through the air. His sack went sailing off in another direction. A snowdrift broke his fall somewhat, and he managed to scramble up and start to run, hearing the Blackfoot closing in on him.

The warrior emitted a war cry, and Campbell looked back. The Indian was about to strike with his lance.

Campbell skidded to a stop and whirled almost in one motion. He leaned toward the side suddenly and reached out to grab the lance. He tugged, and pulled the warrior off the pony. As the Blackfoot tried to rise, Campbell kicked him in the face, then plunged the lance through his heart.

Campbell looked back toward the village. The other Blackfeet were approaching. He scooped up his blanket and ran to the Blackfoot's pony. He jumped on and kicked the pony with his heels. He dashed along, heedless of the slippery ground, not worrying about the few supplies he no longer had. He worried now only about making good his escape. He would worry about food and anything else later.

Some hours later—he was not even sure how long it was—Campbell looked behind him. The Blackfeet seemed to have given up their pursuit. Still, he kept the horse moving fast. Finally, the pony stumbled, but regained its balance. It began to falter more frequently, and Campbell knew the animal was near dead. He pulled to a halt and dismounted.

The pony was blowing hard, and its legs were splayed. It didn't look like it could go another step. Campbell pulled his knife and walked toward the horse. "Sorry, lad," he said. "Ye served me well, and ye maybe can do so some more. Besides, I canna stand to see ye suffer so." With one stroke, he slit the horse's neck and then danced out of the way as the animal fell and jerked around in its death throes.

Campbell butchered out some meat and wrapped it in a piece of the horse's hide. Drawing his blanket around him again, he slung the meat over his shoulder and walked off, after checking the stars to get his bearings. He headed south, not sure of where he wanted to go, but figuring that going south would throw the Blackfeet off if they came after him.

Ever fearful of being followed, Campbell pushed himself hard, not stopping to rest or to eat for more than eighteen hours, but finally he could go no longer. He found a grove of trees in which the wind was considerably lessened. A fire, though, was out of the question, he decided. He gnawed at the frozen horse meat, getting a little nourishment from it.

He sat shivering in the cold, feeling miserable. Then he shook himself out of his lethargy and began moving around, trying to raise his temperature a little. He hacked off a good stack of pine branches and then scraped away the snow from a spot where it wasn't too deep. He laid down some of the branches, lay down on them, bringing his hide-wrapped package of horse meat with him, and then covered himself with the rest of the branches.

Campbell dozed off, but woke often, shivering. It snowed during the night. The flakes covered him and served to insulate him some. He awoke near dawn, teeth chattering. He was damp, shaking and cold. "Damn," he swore as he forced himself out of his bed. He ached in every joint and muscle. He felt desultory and almost disoriented.

"Fuck those Blackfeet," he suddenly said. "Let them come." He found a handful of dry pine needles and some twigs, plus bigger wood. He took two sticks and tied one of his few remaining fringes to each end of one. He wound the fringe around the other stick and worked with the bow to get a fire going. It took a while, but he finally managed.

As he put the horse meat in the fire to cook, he sat there rubbing his hands. It was amazing, he thought, how a simple pleasure like warming one's hands at a fire could completely change one's outlook. The heated

meat helped even more as he wolfed down great baits
of the tough flesh.

Stomach almost full, he gathered his branches
and made a bed right near the fire, which he built up.
He spread his thin blanket on the branches, lay down
again, pulled the blanket around him and then tugged
on the rest of the branches. He fell asleep almost
instantly.

19

There seemed to be no pursuit when Campbell finally pushed on, and he was relieved. He was also a little baffled. As much as Talking Wolf hated him, he figured the Blackfeet would not give up until they had him again. That thought worried him, for he knew that Talking Wolf would be enraged, and that his stay in the village the next time would be even worse than the last.

Campbell wondered if perhaps they turned back to get up an even larger war party, and to get supplies. Then they would be able to easily run him down.

He finally decided, though, that Talking Wolf was worried about his family and the others in his village, and that the warriors had turned back to wait out the winter. Campbell was sure the Blackfeet would be coming for him again in the spring. That worried him, too, but it also made him a little glad. If they found him—and he was certain they would—Talking Wolf would be in for a surprise, Campbell vowed. He would end it once and for all.

A few days after his escape, Campbell turned west and a little south. He did not know any other way to go. There was nothing to the east, as far as he knew, except Blackfeet. To the south lay only God knew what, really. Campbell had the notion that there were plenty of Indians down that way, and not all of them would be friendly to a lone white man tramping through their lands. There might also be Blackfeet down that way, too. Northward lay Canada, which he knew nothing about, other than having heard that it was an even emptier land than where he was traveling now. To the west or southwest, though, were Sharp and Finch, if they were still alive. Morning Sun was that way, too. So were the Nez Percé. And probably other trappers. He thought he might get lucky and find a large camp of trappers, one large enough to withstand a Blackfoot attack, if indeed those warriors were coming after him.

He had left that morning amid some snow flurries that grew steadily heavier as the day wore on. By early afternoon, he was struggling through a raging snowstorm. The howling, screaming wind pushed the snow into fine particles that bit at his face and cut through his thin blanket and clothes.

Campbell continued, having little choice. He was out in the open, with no shelter in sight. The small groves of trees and brush along riverbanks were few and far between. His legs ached from plowing through ever-deepening snow, and he was chilled right down to the bone. He did not think he would ever be warm again. The icy wetness soaked through his moccasins, even though he had lined them with fur, and his pants legs, adding to his misery. Snow melted and trickled down the back of his neck.

He thought frequently of giving up; of just falling to the ground and surrendering to the elements and fate. It would be so easy, so comfortable, so sensible. But he always growled at himself and snarled through gritted teeth, "Nae, I willna do it." Still he plunged on, the activity keeping him from freezing to death, inertia driving him forward one agonizing step after another.

He was not really sure when night fell. It had been dark under the clouds during the day, and he was half in a daze anyway. He just became aware at some point that the sun, however feeble and blocked, was no longer up. He slogged on, wet, cold and wretched.

His luck, such as it was, held, and he finally found another clump of trees. The storm showed no sign yet of abating, but it was almost peaceful in the small stand of cottonwoods and brush. Moving in small, lurching steps, he gathered a little firewood. He scraped some punk from a dead tree and piled it on a piece of bark in a spot he had cleared of snow. He took his fire-bow and set the one stick in the midst of the punk on the bark. Then he furiously began working the bow back and forth, faster and faster. "Come on, laddie," he whispered at one point. "Come on and catch now, damn ye."

A few wisps of smoke curled up, and then a tiny tongue of flame caught on the punk. Campbell tossed the fire-bow aside, grabbed some twigs and piled them gently on the punk. He carefully added larger twigs as the first ones caught. Finally he was able to add a short log about eight inches around. He laughed happily as he held his hands near the flames. Soon after, he stuck his feet near the fire for a bit, grimacing as the heat made them hurt a little after all the cold.

Campbell had a little of the horse meat left, and he tossed it into the flames. His spirits rose as the aroma of the stringy, old flesh began to waft over him. He did not wait long before stabbing the meat and gnawing pieces off it. He felt strength returning to his body. "Aye, laddie," he said softly when he had eaten half the meat, "ye may just make it after all."

He forced himself to save the other half of the meat—just about enough for one more meal. He slept that night almost curled around the fire. He woke periodically as one side of him got too hot and the other too cold. He would reverse his position and drift off again.

It was bitter, frigid cold when he awoke shortly after dawn, since the fire had died down considerably, but the snow had stopped and the day was light gray. He gathered more wood and built up the fire, heated the last of the meat and ate it.

Loath to leave the fire, he lingered, indulging himself a little. He knew he should press on, but the thought was daunting. He wished he could carry a few hot coals with him, not only to keep himself warm on the journey but also to make it easier starting a fire. He could not, though, and he finally forced himself to push out across the vast white expanse. The clouds were still heavy overhead, and Campbell worried that it might begin to snow again. It did, but it was only sporadic and light.

He found no shelter that night and struggled on as long as he could. He finally collapsed in a heap in the snow. He slept fitfully, the cold keeping him awake most of the time, and his fear of freezing to death doing the rest. In the morning he walked on, woodenly crunching through the thin coating of ice on the knee-deep snow.

As the afternoon waned, the sun broke through the clouds, bright and clear. It had little effect on the temperature, though. He did find another small stand of trees and again made himself a fire. His stomach growled and made odd noises.

He was so tired that sleep was fairly easy in coming. His slumber, though, was disturbed, hunger making him restless. He set off in the morning with sinking spirits. "Ye must find yoursel' some food, laddie," he muttered as he plunged on. "And soon."

He had taken to talking to himself more and more, but he was not concerned about that. He figured he either did that or he would lose his reason, something he grudgingly admitted might have already happened.

The sun was bright this day, glaring off the snow and ice so much that it hurt. As he walked on and on, he realized he was beginning to have trouble seeing. "Damn," he yelled, concluding that he was going snow-blind. Hastily he sliced off a strip of his blanket and pierced two slits in it. He tied the thing around his head so he could see through the slits.

"Aye, 'tis much better," he said, resuming his march.

Though it was no longer snowing, the wind had picked up again, whipping at him. It bit right through him, chilling him until he had trouble walking. Once again he wanted nothing more than to just stop here and fall, to die peacefully in the cold.

He forced his mind into blankness, seeing little but the white emptiness before him. He was heading up into the mountains now, and so he focused on one small peak a way ahead and automatically placed one foot in front of the other, oblivious to everything around him except that peak, until even that faded into the oblivion of his blank mind.

It suddenly dawned on him that darkness had fallen. In his state of mind, he had not noticed for some time. He could find no trees, though he did manage to spot a boulder. He hunched on its leeward side, grateful that it blocked out most of the wind. It did little for the cold, though. Campbell had a rough night, and he was still in a semi-stupor when he set out again in the morning.

Hunger still gnawed and clawed at his belly, but he ignored it as he did everything else. With eyes covered by the strip of blanket, fixed straight ahead, he clumped slowly on, focusing on nothing but the next step. The peak he had locked on had become obscured by the steepening climb, and he was forced to shift his gaze from rock to tree to peak to trail, such as it was. He saw none of it, really.

The next two days were the same—a blur of snow, ice, hunger, cold and pain. He lost virtually all touch with reality, snapping out of his haze only rarely. He stumbled often and fell numerous times.

Four days after leaving his last fire, Campbell spotted something in the distance. He had focused on nothing for three days, and the incongruity was enough to partially bring him out of his stupor. The sight, he realized, was accompanied by strange sounds.

He pushed himself a little harder, trying to hurry. As he neared the vision, he could see moving figures. It took some moments to realize what they were. "Wolves!" he muttered. Worry clutched at him. He had nowhere near the strength to fight them off if the animals decided to attack him.

That seemed unlikely, though, since he realized they were tearing apart the carcass of an elk. Hunger and the sight of the meat pushed his fear back and down. Gathering his last reserves, Campbell ran as well as he could toward the wolves. He flapped his arms and screeched at the top of his lungs. The wolves turned to snarl at him, but this flapping, screaming demon finally frightened them off. They ran, howling and yapping, but they did not go far. They circled back to pad back and forth forty yards away, snarling and watching this curious apparition.

The carcass was still warm. With his knife, Campbell enlarged the gash the wolves had created in the animal's belly cavity. He wrenched out the liver and ate it raw, luxuriating in its taste and heat. He swallowed the meat almost without chewing.

His stomach revolted at the unaccustomed meat, and Campbell fought hard to keep his gorge down. He succeeded, but it made him realize he would have to go easy on this newfound food, at least until he was acclimated to having something in his stomach again. He carefully cut the elk's hide off, nibbling at the liver as he worked.

Wrapping the hide around his shoulders on top of the blanket—bloody side outward—he fastened both closed with slivers hacked from the elk's antlers. He felt a little warmer immediately, and he grinned. He looked over at the wolves still pacing nearby. "Ye lads have saved my life," he said to them, "and I thank ye wholesomely for it."

Campbell butchered as much meat as he thought he could carry. He cut a strip from the bottom of the elk skin and tied it around the meat. He slung it over his shoulder and started moving off. As he did, he looked to the wolves again. "Since ye laddies have saved me, I willna take all your food. Ye can have the rest and it should be plenty for ye."

He trudged off, a new spring in his step. He turned to look back after a few paces and saw the wolves already creeping back toward the carcass. In moments he could hear them tearing at it again.

Up out of the plains and foothills, he found more trees, and that served to lighten his mood even more. He even managed to sing an airy, lilting tune from his homeland as he walked, though within minutes he was wheezing and panting. He gave up the song.

Campbell found shelter that night in a stand of trees that faced a mountain meadow. He built himself a good fire, hacked off some pieces of frozen elk meat and cooked them for a bit. The first two he ate were still cold and raw on the inside, but he didn't care. Once those were down in his stomach, though, he sat back a little and allowed the rest of the meat he had put in the fire to cook more thoroughly.

As he sat by the warm blaze, he worked on the elk hide, scraping the fat and gristle off it with his knife. He wrapped it around a tree then and tugged it back and forth, rubbing it on the rough tree bark to clean it more and soften it some. By then, he was exhausted, and he built up the fire. Then he stretched out, close to the fire, and wrapped himself in his blanket and elk skin to sleep.

He ate well in the morning and smoked the elk hide some to cure it. He did the same the next day and the morning after that. Then he trudged off again. For the first time since he had fled the Blackfoot village, he thought he might have a chance to survive, though he still had God knew how many miles to go before he found anyone.

It started snowing again just after he left, in big, soft, wet flakes. Campbell adjusted the elk skin, pulling it over his head and repinning it. It kept the snow from melting down his neck and with the blanket he was almost warm.

As the day lengthened, the wind picked up and the snow changed from thick, fat flakes to small, stinging particles. The wind whistled around him, whipping the ends of the elk hide into a frenzied dance.

The snow crusted over with ice almost as soon as it landed, or so it seemed to Campbell. With each step, he would break through the crust and sink into the snow, slowing him down to almost next to nothing. His feet were soon numb and his legs leaden. But he pushed on, though he could feel himself weakening fast. He fought to keep himself alert, watching for any place he might find shelter.

He finally found a good-sized grove of aspens and pines. With renewed vigor, he built a fire and then gathered a decent amount of wood. He was not planning to go anywhere for a while. He needed to rest and recover as much as he could before tackling the rest of his journey. During his walk today, he had felt the ground rising steeply, and he knew he would be heading deep into the mountains now. He would need whatever strength he could muster for that.

He stayed for two days, eating elk almost constantly, and keeping near to the fire to stay warm. The snowstorm roared around him the whole time, seemingly never easing at all. But he was warm and his belly mostly filled. Sheltered for the most part from the storm, he felt reasonably good.

The next morning broke bright and cold, the storm having petered out during the night. The whiteness was dazzling in the sunlight. He ate the last of the elk, covered his eyes with the strip of blanket, pulled his blanket and elk skin around him and trudged off. He was singing again.

The next four days were the worst he had had. His feet bled from being cut each time he broke through the ice. His moccasins were cut and worn. He tried to patch them with pieces cut from the elk hide, but they still wore through rapidly.

Without food, he suffered all the more. On the second day, he was staggering along in a semi-stupor, unaware of the trail of blood droplets he left behind in the snow. He was mostly unaware, too, of his bleeding hands and arms, cut during the many times he fell and his hands broke the ice crust.

About the only bright spot was that he always found shelter in trees. He also managed to make a fire every night. That helped him warm up, and let him face each day with at least a minimum of hope. That, however, wore off within minutes of his leaving each day.

Despite his despair, something inside kept him moving, driving him ahead, across meadows, through snow-clogged passes. It was all unconscious, though. He did not know of his pains or where he was going. He did not know about the pack of wolves that had started following him on the third day out. He just plunged on, moving one foot woodenly ahead of the other.

20

"Cap'n Bridger! Someone's comin'."

Ol' Gabe Bridger stepped out of his canvas-wall tent. His thick, knee-length moccasins crunched on the snow as he walked toward the guard who had called out to him. Other men of his brigade, all armed, were warily following. "What's doin's, Riley?" Bridger asked.

"Out there, Cap'n," Otis Riley said, pointing to the far side of the meadow, where a figure had shuffled out of the trees. "Looks like a goddamn redskin."

Bridger stood there staring. There seemed to be no danger, unless some Blackfeet had sent this old-looking figure out as some kind of decoy. Bridger walked out a little farther, still staring. Jim Bridger had better eyesight than most men, and his trappers knew it. Suddenly he turned. "Patterson, Baker," he ordered "go out thar and help that poor ol' hoss in hyar."

"But Cap'n . . ." Sam Patterson started.

"Don't give me no shit, hoss," Bridger growled. He was not a man who liked having his orders questioned.

"But suppose there're other Injuns back in them trees," Patterson said, not sure if he was more afraid of that or of incurring Bridger's wrath.

"That ain't no Injun, boy," Bridger said roughly.

"You sure, Cap'n?" Patterson asked.

Bridger was not pleased with Patterson. The man had been a thorn in his side since leaving rendezvous. He was too fainthearted for the life of a trapper. "Ain't no Injun I ary saw wore a full beard, boy," he snapped. "Now git movin'."

The two men jumped bareback on horses that others had put Indian-style reins on, and rode out toward the solitary, bent figure. They pulled to a stop near the man, who did not look up. Baker dismounted and handed his rein to Patterson. He moved up and put a hand on the man's shoulder.

Campbell stopped but stood staring straight ahead.

Baker looked up at Patterson. "This chil's in some poor shape," he said. He looked back at Campbell. "Hey, hoss, what's your name?"

Campbell did not move. Baker shook him gently. "Come on now, hoss, snap out of it. We're here to help ya."

Campbell slowly swiveled his head and looked at the trapper's face, though he did not really see it. Then he collapsed, falling in a heap at Baker's feet.

"Goddamn," Baker muttered, "this chil's more dead than alive." He jammed the butt of his rifle into the snow, then knelt and tried to lift Campbell. Though Campbell had gaunted down considerably, he was still a pretty big man, and Baker could not manage it. Puffing, he looked up at Patterson. "Well come on down here, and give me a hand, goddammit," he snapped.

Patterson grimaced. "What about the horses?" he countered.

"They ain't goin' nowhere. Now come on, before we freeze our asses off out here in the open like this."

Patterson still didn't like it, but did as he was told. He, too, jammed the butt of his rifle in the snow. Then the two lifted Campbell and placed him across the horse Baker had used. Patterson mounted his own horse again. "You're aimin' to walk back, ain't ya?" he asked.

Baker looked at him, annoyed. He had planned so, but he thought it might've been a decent gesture for Patterson to have offered to let him ride double. "Yes, goddammit, go on hurry back to the others." He was only a little surprised when Patterson took him literally and trotted off. "Fuckin' idiot," Baker muttered.

Baker took the rope rein to the horse and tugged it forward. He walked slowly back toward the big trappers' camp. When he got there, he found that Patterson had, at least, explained a little. Several men eased Campbell off the horse and carried him into Bridger's tent and placed him on Bridger's cot, near the small camp stove.

Bridger came in and looked down. "Good Christ," he whispered as he got a good look at the man on the cot, "that's the chil' won my rifle down at rendezvous."

"He looks plumb bad, Cap'n," one of the men said.

Bridger nodded. "Where's Doc?" he asked.

"Right here, Cap'n," Robert Newell said as he shoved forward. "Now get the hell out of the way so's I can take a look at him." Newell was not a real physician, but his success in doctoring trappers had earned him that nickname. And he knew more about such things than any of the others did.

Newell cut away Campbell's clothes as easily and quickly as they could. Campbell's odor was bad, even to the rank trappers.

"He sure is a sight," one man said.

Newell just grunted, immersed in his work. When he had Campbell undressed, he looked him over swiftly. Then he covered Campbell with a blanket and looked up at Bridger. "I don't know where this hoss's been or what he's been through, but I'm surprised he ain't dead. As far as I can tell, he's got some frostbite, ague, probably pneumonia, malnutrition, and he's been exposed to the elements far too long."

"Think he'll live?" Bridger had taken a shine to the young Scotsman at rendezvous and somehow felt responsible for him.

"Hell if I know, Cap'n. Most ordinary men, I'd say no. But he don't seem so ordinary, if I remember from rendezvous. It could go either way. I figure that if he can make it through the next few days, he ought to be all right."

Bridger nodded. "Do all you can for him, Doc," he said. "Leave him in here where it's warm. I'll throw my robes in with Meek." With a last look at Campbell and a sad shake of the head, he turned and left.

The other men followed him, leaving Newell alone with his patient.

Newell stayed with Campbell, sleeping on blankets on the floor next to the cot. He had his doubts that he could help the young man, seeing as how he wasn't really a doctor. He wasn't even sure that a real doctor could do him any good. Still, he had to try.

Campbell awoke periodically but did not show

any signs of reason or recognition. He rambled in delirium at times, shouting snatches of sentences that no one could understand. He tossed and turned and flopped, thrashing about so much at times that he had to be secured down.

During the infrequent, short periods when Campbell was awake, Newell would force as much warm soup down his throat as possible, figuring the nourishment would do some good. He kept Campbell bundled up in blankets and poulticed the cuts frequently.

Nine days after he had been spotted just outside Bridger's camp, Campbell awoke for real. His eyes focused and he looked around.

Newell was sitting against a willow backrest nearby. He saw Campbell moving and noticed that it seemed different. He stood and stepped to the cot. Seeing Campbell's eyes open, Newell said, "How's doin's, ol' beaver?"

"Shinin'," Campbell said, trying to be sarcastic but not sure he had accomplished it.

"I misdoubt that, boy," Newell said with a grin.

"Where am I?" Campbell asked.

"Ol' Gabe's camp. On the Blackfoot River, in a valley at the southern edge of the Flatheads."

"Gabe Bridger's camp?" Campbell asked, surprised.

"Yep. Gabe says he knows you."

Campbell nodded weakly. "I won his rifle back at rendezvous." He paused, licked his lips, sighed. "How'd I get here?"

Newell shrugged. "One of the guards spotted you comin' out of the woods across the meadow. When we determined you were a white man, a couple of the boys went out there and got you and brought you here. And, before ya ask, you've been here nine days."

Campbell nodded again. "Who're you?" he asked.

"Bob Newell. Most of the critters in these parts call me Doc."

"Are ye?"

"Closest thing you'll see to one out here, hoss."

"I canna express my thanks for pullin' me through, Doc," Campbell said. "If there's e'er anythin' I can do for ye . . . "

"You can start by tellin' me your name."

"Of course. My head does nae seem to be workin' very well these days. Alexander Campbell."

"Think you're up for a little more talkin'? I expect Gabe'll want to hear your story."

"I dunna think I can do much more, Doc. I'm sorry."

"No need to apologize, boy. You've been through some rough doin's. Can ya eat some?"

"Aye," Campbell said with as much enthusiasm as he could muster.

Newell poured as much soup and coffee into Campbell as he thought the Scotsman could take, then told him to sleep some more. For the first time since having gotten his patient, Newell left the tent for more than the few minutes necessary to take care of personal needs. He reported to Bridger, then went and got himself some sleep.

The next time Campbell awoke, Newell was there again. The doctor sent for Bridger immediately.

"How's doin's, ol' hoss?" Bridger said with a grin as he squatted by the cot. Snow melted and dripped off his blanket coat.

"Better than I was, Mister Bridger."

"Gabe, remember? Ye had us worried, hoss. When we found ye, ye was more dead than alive. Where'd ye come from?"

"Blackfoot camp up on the Milk River."

"Waugh!" Bridger grunted. "On foot? That's more'n two hundred miles, most of it through mountains; and in the worst of winter, too."

"On foot, aye," Campbell said. "There was many a time I dinna think I'd e'er see another day."

"Well, ye did make it another day, boy. And ye ain't gonna go under on us now. Doc'll have your hide, ye pull that shit on him." He grinned again, and was rewarded by a weak smile from the patient. "What was ye doin' in a Blackfoot camp, boy?" Bridger asked after a few moments' silence.

"I was taken prisoner by those red devils just after Christmas. Me and Caleb and Ethan had just set up a winter camp up on the Coeur d'Alene. We were trappin' individually. Next thing I know, a bunch of Blackfeet popped up out of the brush. I winged one, but then they were all o'er me." He shrugged.

"Ethan and Caleb?"

Campbell shrugged again. "I haven't seen them since that mornin'. I hope they're safe."

"Ye didn't see 'em in that Blackfoot village?"

"Nae. Nor on the ride out there. I'm hopin' the Blackfeet dinna bother them."

"Seems like a lot of trouble for Bug's Boys to drag your scrawny Scot's ass all the way across the Bitterroots and the Flatheads jist for the hell of it," Bridger noted.

"Aye. The one who took me—a lovely son of a bitch named Talkin' Wolf—told me he wanted me to suffer for killin' his son in that battle on the way to rendezvous last year. To do that, he gave me o'er to an old man and his two ancient wives for bein' their slave. The ol' man sort of took somethin' of a likin' to me and began talkin' about havin' me adopted into the band. I dinna want that anyway, but Talkin' Wolf was nae going to let that happen in any case. I knew I'd be in even worse trouble the longer I stayed, so I made my escape."

"Black-hearted bastard," Bridger said with feeling.

"Aye, he's that, all right."

"Look's like ye faced some doin's, boy."

"I did what I had to. But I was nae sure I was going to find any help."

Bridger's lips twitched in something of a smile. "And my rifle?" he asked. "Or, ruther, your rifle, hoss?" he corrected himself.

"Talkin' Wolf has it," Campbell said sourly. "But I'll nae let him keep it. I'll get it back one day."

Bridger nodded and patted Campbell's nearest arm. "Well, ol' hoss, ye did it. You're here now and safe. Ye jist worry about gettin' yourself on the mend. You git well, and you're more'n welcome to join my outfit hyar. Same terms as any of the others."

"Thank ye, Gabe. I'll have to think about it, though."

Bridger nodded. "I ain't in no rush, hoss." He grinned. "Unless ye plan on takin' till summer to git back on your feet."

"I dunna think it'll be that long," Campbell said firmly. "And if it does take that long, ye and your men can leave me here. I'll make my way as best I can when I can."

"Ain't likely, hoss," Bridger growled, eyes narrowing in anger. "We'll cart ye along in a litter if'n we have to."

Campbell was a little surprised by Bridger's anger. But he didn't know about the time Bridger and another man had been left to wait for another in their party to die before they could bury him. But the old man who was with Bridger had talked the eighteen-year-old into just rolling the wounded man into a hole and leaving with all his possessions. The man had lived and had hunted Bridger and his companion down. He let them live, but Bridger had vowed then and there not to ever again do something like that.

21

Campbell progressed quickly, and within another week he was eating solid food, increasing his intake regularly. A week after that, he finally got out of the cot. With the help of two men, he managed to walk a few steps. A few days after that, he was walking by himself. It was slow and hesitant, but it was under his own power. He gained strength and vigor fairly rapidly, and as soon as he could, he began helping the men in camp with their chores. He wanted to pay them back, in some small way, for having saved his life.

Spring finally approached. Not all at once, of course, but with a gradual warming and the beginnings of greenery. With the new season looming, Bridger was ready to move his camp. At the same time, Campbell was eager to be on the move, too, but he was looking to the west. He wanted to find Finch and Sharp, but most important, he wanted to find Morning Sun.

One fine morning, he went to Bridger. "I canna

thank ye and your men enough, Cap'n," he said, having fallen into calling Bridger by the sobriquet his other men used.

"'Tweren't nothin', boy. Ye seem fit now. Are ye ready to join up with us?"

Campbell was uncomfortable. He did not want Bridger to see him as unappreciative. "I'm grateful for the offer, Cap'n, but I think I'll nae do it." He tried to ignore Bridger's surprise and continued. "I was wonderin' what the chance was of ye lettin' me have a little bit in the way of supplies. On credit. I'll pay ye back at rendezvous, or if I canna get enough plews for that, I'll do it at the rendezvous the year after."

"What for?" Bridger asked, still surprised.

Campbell half smiled. "I miss my woman, Cap'n. I want to find her. And my two friends, Caleb and Ethan. I figure I can make it to the Nay Percy village on my own. If they're alive and well, they'll head there, too. If they're not . . ." He shrugged his shoulders, not wanting to consider that possibility.

"I could use a good hand like ye, Alex," Bridger said seriously. "Some of those hosses out there don't shine for shit. You're a chil's got some sand in him. Ye proved that easy enough when ye come through all ye did with them Blackfeet. Ain't too many critters out there could do the same."

"I know ye can, Cap'n. But ye've plenty of boys wi' ye." He paused, thinking. "I dunna want ye thinkin' I'm ungrateful for all ye've done for me, but I really need to find my friends, and my woman. I'll tell ye what, though, ye give me some supplies. If I canna pay ye back at rendezvous this summer, I'll hire on to ye for the next season."

"And leave Ethan and Caleb behind?"

"Aye." Campbell paused again, trying to think of how to phrase this. "They're my friends, no doubt about that. I canna change it. But I'd be in your debt, and it's more important to me to pay that back. Ye told me when I won your rifle that ye'd ne'er gone back on payin' a wager. Well, Cap'n, I don't think I e'er went off owin' someone somethin' with no intention of payin'. I'll also tell ye this: If ye dunna like the idea of givin' me supplies and lettin' me ride off on me own, and if ye think I'm not bein' properly grateful to ye if I were to do that, then I'll stay here as one of your hired men."

"Ye would, wouldn't ye?" Bridger looked sharply at him.

"Aye."

Bridger believed him. He nodded. "We can outfit ye, boy," he said gruffly. "But we can't spare too much."

"I understand," Campbell said, battling down his excitement.

"When're ye fixin' to leave, boy?"

"Next day or two. I'm itchy to be on the move."

Bridger laughed. "I know that feelin', ol' hoss." He paused. "Ye come by in the mornin'. We'll cut ye out a decent horse and a mule, maybe, and see what supplies ye need."

"I dunna want to put ye out too much, Cap'n. A horse'll do just fine. Or a mule, if ye'd rather keep your horses."

"Don't ye argue with me, goddammit," Bridger growled in mock anger.

Campbell nodded. "I dunna know how to thank ye, Cap'n."

"I know one way, hoss," Bridger said flatly. "Kill some goddamn Blackfeet for me if ye ary git the chance." When he saw Campbell's raised eyebrows, he nodded. "I hate 'em, too, boy. Bastards put an arrow in my back three goddamn years ago. Goddamn thing's still there. Pains me somethin' awful every now and again. Shit-eaters."

"That's an easy enough thing to do, Cap'n," Campbell said. He fully intended to kill some Blackfeet for himself. They would have to be paid back for the trouble, pain and humiliation they had heaped on him. And if they had killed Finch, Sharp, or Morning Sun, there would be even more hell for the Blackfeet to pay, he vowed.

Two days later, Campbell rode out on a big bay mare, trailing a mule loaded with supplies behind him. Bridger had given him enough food to last a month, if he watched himself with it; a few trade goods, just in case; a new outfit of buckskins; a short, warm wool capote; a tomahawk; trade musket; pistol; a little tobacco; some powder and ball.

He headed almost due west, toward Lolo Pass, figuring to look for Tall Clouds's village of Nez Percé. If he couldn't find them where they usually were at this time of year, then he would head for rendezvous. They would surely be there, as would Finch, Sharp, and the women—if they were alive.

Traveling was slow, since he still got snow every once in a while. And, while he was in a rush because he wanted to see Morning Sun, he had sense enough not to push too hard. He was not yet as fully recovered as he could be, and he didn't want to risk losing one of the animals. So he took his time without delaying too much. He tired easily for the first few days, until he got used to traveling again.

The journey was a lot easier than his earlier one had been, he thought frequently as he rode through mountain valleys and still-snowy meadows. He stopped at the hot springs just east of Lolo Pass and immersed himself in the healing waters there, resting for two days. He felt like a new man when he rode on again.

Lolo Pass was still thick with snow, but didn't delay him too much. He stopped for a couple of days on the west side of the pass to allow the horse and mule to rest a little.

Twenty-two days after leaving Bridger's camp, Campbell was following the Lochsa River. As he approached its confluence with the Selway River, he saw smoke, and he stopped, watching intently. There was not much smoke, and not too many scavenger birds were flying around, so he figured it was not an Indian village. It was the camp of a small party, that much he knew. But who? It could be a hunting party of Flatheads or Bannacks, or even Nez Percé. It could be a war party of any of those Indians. Or it could be a war party of Blackfeet.

He shook his head in annoyance at letting his mind get carried away. It could very well be a party of trappers. Maybe even Finch and Sharp, though if it was them, the camp seemed mighty small. Even if it were Flatheads or Bannacks, they were friendly to white men, and probably wouldn't bother him much.

With a shrug, he rode on, heading toward the camp. As he worked his way through the trees and such, and the camp became more visible, he saw canvas tents, and knew right off it was white men. It was a disappointment, since he knew it was not his two partners, and therefore, Morning Sun was not around. Once he got used to that thought, it was something of a relief. He could do with a little companionship.

Moments later, he jerked his horse to a halt. He sat

there, letting his feelings and emotions sort themselves out. He knew the best thing he could do was to just ride away, go back the way he had come a little way and then skirt the camp. Trouble was, he couldn't. He had gone through too much, faced too many obstacles, endured too much pain to just walk away from this camp.

He scratched his fluffy red beard a moment, and then decided. He dismounted and tied his horse and mule to the trees. He eased his musket out of the saddle scabbard and checked its priming. He also checked his pistol and shoved it back into his belt, which he wore outside his capote. The day was cool, crisp, with the fresh scent of new growth in the air. He turned and started walking with long strides toward the camp.

Alexander Campbell had learned a lot in his two years in the mountains. One of them was the ability to walk silently when it was needed. It was not a conscious thing, he just did it, moving like a spirit through the trees.

No one noticed him when he entered the camp, which suited his purposes just fine. One man was sitting on a log with his back to Campbell, only ten yards away. Without remorse, Campbell shot Val Knebel in the back of the head with the rifle. Then he tossed the rifle aside.

Knebel never knew what hit him. He simply got shoved forward onto his face, which landed in a small fire there.

"What the . . . ?" Juan Acosta said as he stumbled out of a tent fifteen feet away. He spotted Campbell and his eyes grew wide.

Campbell calmly pulled his pistol, palmed the hammer back and shot Acosta in the throat. The Mexican grabbed his neck and tried to shout, but his voice box would not work. Blood sprayed out of his mouth and throat. He half spun and fell, grabbing a corner of the tent as he did. Half the tent collapsed.

Campbell shoved the pistol away as he spotted Simon Beesley coming around the far side of the other tent twenty feet away.

"Who the fuck're you?" Beesley demanded as he reached for his pistol.

Campbell pulled his tomahawk and threw it. He didn't want to kill Beesley with it; just wanted to throw Beesley's shot off. He succeeded. Campbell was already running, though, and by the time the tomahawk glanced off Beesley's shoulder, Campbell was almost on top of the man. Campbell flung himself forward, and brought Beesley down, landing on top of him. He began pounding the man in the face.

Campbell noticed as he thumped Beesley that he no longer looked so dangerous; not nearly as dangerous as he had seemed when Campbell had first encountered him in Independence two years ago.

Campbell finally quit pelting the man. He stood, dragging Beesley with him. Beesley still had long, greasy hair and his face was still gaunt under the old dirt and fresh blood and bruises. He didn't seem as big to Campbell, but his eyes still gave him a furtive appearance. Campbell shoved Beesley backward. He stumbled and fell on his seat, back almost up against a tree. Campbell picked up his tomahawk and squatted in front of Beesley.

"Who the fuck're you?" Beesley asked again.

"Ye dunna know who I am, laddie?" Campbell countered.

"No. Not unless you're . . . Jesus fuckin' Christ, you are him, ain't you? That goddamn murderin' Scotsman."

"Aye, laddie," Campbell said harshly. "The one

ye left to die out there in the midst of nowhere, at the mercy of the savage Indians and the savage beasties. I dinna think I'd e'er find ye again."

"Hey, come on, hoss," Beesley said nervously, "you cain't hold that agin me. After all, you kilt one of my boys. I had to do somethin'."

"Then ye should've come against me face-to-face, ye clap-ridden clod."

"Well, I wanted to," Beesley whined, "but the others didn't."

"Ye be full of shit, laddie," Campbell said unmercifully. "Ye have no balls, no courage, no honor. Aye, ye're a chicken-spirited laddie, ye are."

"What're you gonna do with me?"

"What do ye think? Or maybe I should ask ye if ye can think?"

"I think you're gonna kill me," Beesley said, fear deep and strong in his guts.

"Aye, laddie. That I plan to do."

"Anything I can do to change your mind, hoss?"

"I dunna think so." Campbell tapped the flat side of his tomahawk blade on his left hand.

"Wait! Wait a goddamn minute now, hoss," Beesley said desperately. "There's gotta be somethin' we can do hyar. How's about this. I'll give ya all our plews. Ever' goddamn last fuckin' one of 'em."

Campbell had not considered that possibility, but now it seemed logical. Thing is, he had no plans of letting Beesley go free, plews or not. The thought of the empty plains, the possibility of Indian attack, the fact that he had wandered around not knowing where he was or where he was going kept Campbell angry. This man had been responsible for all that.

"That might be workable," he lied. "What else?"

"Anything we got here. Jist leave me enough to make it down to rendezvous with my hair."

"Why should I do that?"

"You're doin' all right for yourself, ain't ya?" Beesley countered. "Ye look pretty good, and you're still up in the mountains after two years. I bet you've even got yourself some hot little squaw packed away some place, don't ya?" He winked in manly fellow lechery.

That was true, Campbell figured. If Beesley hadn't left him out on the plains by himself, he never would've stumbled on Finch and Sharp, and therefore never would've met Morning Sun. Of course, they could all be dead now and that didn't please him. Still, it made him reconsider killing Beesley. "Aye, I have a woman," he allowed. Then he grew silent again.

"How'd you come to be in the mountains anyway?"

"I was found by a couple of trappers. They took me in."

"Who?"

"Caleb Finch and Ethan Sharp."

"Cain't say as I know 'em."

Campbell shrugged. He stood, still wondering whether he really should kill Beesley. He paced a little in front of Beesley and then walked away a few feet, thoughts dulling his alertness.

Suddenly he heard something behind him, and he whirled, throwing the tomahawk at the same time. This time he was trying for a hit. Once again he succeeded. The blade bit into Beesley's chest. Beesley dropped his knife.

Campbell walked over and jerked the weapon out of Beesley, who was still alive. "Goddamn fool," Campbell muttered. Then he cleaved Beesley's head.

22

Finch and Sharp had little trouble following the trail from where Campbell had been taken. The tracks of six unshod ponies, plus an occasional splatter of blood made it relatively easy. Still, it was slow going, since they had to keep a constant watch on where they were going. Patches of rock or new snow or small brooks might wipe out the trail for a bit, and they would have to spend a few minutes searching for it. When they started, they were only a few minutes behind the Blackfeet, they figured. By the time they had been out an hour, they figured they were close to that much behind them.

They hit a large section of rock swept bare of snow by the harsh wind, and the tracks were lost. "Shit," Finch muttered. "Ye circle 'round to the south and east," he said to Sharp. "I'll head the other way. Maybe we can cut their trail again afore long."

They lost more than another hour of precious time before Finch heard Sharp fire his rifle. He galloped toward the sound, and soon spotted his friend kneeling. "What'd ye find?" he asked as he hopped off his horse.

"Horse shit. I figure it's from them."

Finch knelt and touched the horse droppings. "Ain't but two, maybe three hours old," he said.

"I figured about the same. But those boys're movin' fast."

Finch nodded. "It's comin' on close to dark, too," he said. "Well, we ain't gettin' nowhere jist settin' here jawin'. Let's ride."

They moved out again, but within half an hour dusk was falling, making tracking difficult. Finally Sharp stopped. "We'd best give it up for the night, Caleb." He pointed. "That looks like a good spot to stay."

"Reckon you're right."

They rode to the small stand of trees and set about doing their chores. Before long the horses and mule were taken care of and a fire was going. They ate jerky, which was made palatable only by the fact that they had fresh, strong coffee to wash it down. They ate in silence and afterward lit their pipes.

"I hope we don't get no goddamn snow," Sharp finally said.

"Thinkin' we will?"

"Signs say so. Looks like a norther's headin' this way. I'm hopin' our medicine's strong enough to git it to pass by."

"That'd shine with this ol' coon. It wouldn't shine to have to go trackin' those bastards in a snowstorm."

Finch had trouble sleeping that night. He was a

man of action, and he fretted over his inability to do anything. He had become closer to Campbell than Sharp had, and he blamed himself for Campbell's having been taken. Had it not been for Sharp's level-headedness, he would have continued to ride along throughout the night, relying on his instincts to follow the trail that he could not see in the dark.

He understood Sharp's reasoning, though. If they lost the trail at night, they would have to spend hours trying to pick it up again in the morning. If they ever could. Besides, they needed sleep. If they did catch the Blackfeet, they would need their strength and their wits. It would not be wise to go into battle with a war party of Blackfeet half stupefied from lack of sleep.

The Blackfeet would have to sleep sooner or later, too, Finch knew. If they saw no immediate pursuit, the Blackfeet might call it an early night, especially if they had been running hard for a number of hours.

His thoughts finally calmed, and he drifted off into a deep sleep. It seemed like only minutes, though, before Sharp woke him. Sharp already had the fire built up and the coffee hot.

Finch stood, shivering in the cold. He gratefully took the cup of coffee from Sharp. Then the two wolfed down some jerky. When Finch finished off the last of the coffee, he said, "Let's go."

Sharp just nodded, and within minutes they were on their way again. Dawn was just cracking, sending pink shards of light over the land. It was enough to follow the trail.

They moved steadily, if slowly, throughout the day, never stopping other than for a few minutes of rest now and again. Late in the morning, the wind picked up, and the clouds began to thicken, but the overcast drifted off eventually, dropping only a few snowflakes.

The spotty trail of blood had stopped and the two men had to rely on other signs, which got harder and harder to follow. As a grassy saddle of land they were traversing gave way to more rock, they continually lost the trail and had to search hard to pick it up again.

The delays irritated both men, but Finch more than Sharp. Finch was the more impetuous, and he would grumble and curse during their frenzied searches.

"Don't go gittin' your dander up, hoss," Sharp told Finch more than once. "It's only gonna git worse. We got us a hell of a lot of mountain country to cover yet, and it ain't gonna git no easier."

"Goddammit, Ethan, I know that. But searchin' around lookin' for sign don't shine with this ol' coon. Every time we have to stop for such doin's, those sons of bitches git farther ahead."

"We cain't do nothin' about that, hoss, so jist keep lookin'. The more we set jawin', the worse it's gonna git for Alex."

"Ye think he's gone under, Ethan?"

"I misdoubt it. If'n they were gonna put him under, they would've done so long ago and we would've found the body. I was thinkin' maybe they were gonna make sport with him, but that don't seem likely. Not comin' all this far."

"Make a slave out of him maybe?"

"It's possible, I reckon, but why? It don't make no sense for them to drag him all this way for that neither. 'Course, ye nary can tell jist what goes on in the mind of them red devils."

Finch grunted acknowledgment, and they moved on. The horses picked their way slowly and cautiously up a steep slope. They lost the trail again over the top of it. They circled wider and wider, searching.

Finally they stopped. Finch sat there fuming, but Sharp looked eastward. Then Sharp said, "Ye know, hoss, I think we're wastin' our time with all this tryin' to follow their sign. I figure we ought to jist head that-away." He pointed to a mountain pass to the east.

"Why?"

"Blackfoot country's over there. And them critters're gonna head straight for their land. Winter's on its way, and they'll want to be back in their village. I figure we ought to jist git over there and then start lookin' for sign."

"That shines with this ol' coon. More so than what we been doin'. Let's go."

"It's gittin' dark. Let's find us a place to put up for the night."

"Damn, Ethan, jist when we're fixin' to make some time."

"I ain't aimin' to test that pass in the dark. And the horses've been hard-used."

The next morning, they moved out under thickening clouds. "Looks like snow," Sharp said.

"Damn, am I glad I'm with such a chil' as ye. I'd nary know what to expect out here in the wilds otherwise," Finch said sarcastically.

Sharp grinned, taking no offense. "It's gonna be one hell of a storm, too, I'm sayin'."

"Then we best push on."

They made the best time they could without wearing down the horses. Before midmorning, thick, wet snow started to fall. The two men burrowed themselves a little deeper into their coats and rode on. By noon the clouds were thick and black, and the snowfall had increased considerably. The wind had picked up and was howling around them. The snow covered the ground quickly now, piling up, but Finch and Sharp kept riding, moving more by instinct than anything else, since they couldn't see more than a few feet ahead of them.

Two hours later, Sharp pulled up. "This ain't gonna git us nowhere but gone under," he said.

"Ye figurin' to stop?" Finch asked, not really wanting to give up for the day just yet. They hadn't even come to the pass.

"Well, now, I reckon I am. Soon's we can find a place to hole up. I figure this's gonna turn into one hellacious goddamn storm afore it's through."

Finch wanted to argue, but knew his partner was right. He just nodded and they moved on.

Twenty minutes or so later, they found a stand of pines backed up against a cliff. The stone would stem most of the wind, and the trees would cut some more, as well as keep at least some of the snow off them. Some brush and a little old, brown grass would provide at least a little forage for the horses and mule.

They gathered wood after caring for the horses and then got a fire going. They had been lucky enough to shoot a deer that morning, before the storm had really begun, so they were supplied enough with food for a while. They put coffee and meat on the fire and waited for it to get ready. When it was, they ate silently. Finally, they lit their pipes.

Sharp reached into the small possible bag at his side and pulled out some cards. "How's about some three-card monte, hoss?" he asked.

"Naw, Ethan, I ain't in the mood for such."

"Ye aim to jist set there broodin'?" Sharp demanded.

"The snow'll blow itself out when it's ready, and we can git back to lookin' for Alex."

Finch looked up and grinned. "Well, what're we gonna use for bettin'? Ain't no use playin' monte, or hand or anything else, less'n ye got somethin' to bet with."

"We'll figure out somethin' to use."

The storm still shrieked around them the next morning. Even in their protected camp, the snow was accumulating.

"Looks like this might be worse'n ye thought, ol' coon," Finch said.

"I'm glad we ain't out there in the brunt of it."

"Such doin's wouldn't shine with this ol' coon neither," Finch said. He had resigned himself to sitting out the storm now, and so it was easier to accept their situation.

They passed the time playing cards, cleaning their guns, eating, sharpening knives and tomahawks, and talking.

"Wonder how the women're doin'," Finch said somewhere during the afternoon. At least he thought it was afternoon.

"Probably better off than we are, ol' hoss. Don't ye go frettin' about them. They're able. Morning Sun might be gittin' a bit anxious, but Many Bells and Dancin' Feather'll take care of her."

"I'd a heap rather be back there with them now than be sittin' out in this shit," Finch said with a grin. "This ain't this coon's idea of shinin' times."

"Mine neither." Sharp laughed.

Time dragged on, weighing heavily on them, but

there was little they could do. The snow seemed interminable, and they sometimes thought it would never end.

The storm raged around them for a full three days while they sat huddled near the fire for warmth. They were about out of coffee, and the deer meat was running out, but it had kept them mostly warm and filled. Finally, though, the snow began to taper off, and the wind died down some.

It was afternoon when they walked out to the edge of the trees. "Good Jesus, Ethan, look at it out there," Finch said. "The goddamn snow must be three, four feet deep."

"These doin's don't shine in the goddamn least," Sharp grumbled. "We're in a heap of goddamn trouble here, ol' friend."

"Well, now, that's true. But we cain't give up jist yet. We got to keep on tryin' to find Alex."

"I reckon we do, but goin' out there right now ain't wise. Dawn'll be soon enough."

Finch looked thoughtful, but then gave in.

They passed the rest of the afternoon making snowshoes out of the poor materials at hand. It would be a long, tough haul, they knew, as they would have to tramp a path for the horses and mule.

The next morning, they strapped on the snowshoes and tied cloths around their faces, leaving only slits to see out of. They led the two horses and the mule out of the trees and into the stretch of white emptiness broken only by clumps of dark-green pines. They turned east and began tramping down the snow as much as they could, but they still had to drag the animals after them half the time. They flattened down the snow until they were soaking wet and freezing.

They covered less than five miles before darkness caught them.

They found firewood and cooked the last of their deer meat. They had finished their coffee that morning. As he lit his pipe after eating, Sharp said, "I think we best head back, ol' hoss."

"We cain't do that," Finch snapped.

"The idea don't shine much with this ol' hoss neither, Caleb, but we're in deep shit here. All we got left is a little jerky. About enough to git us back to our camp—if our medicine don't git no worse'n it's been. After all this time, Alex is either in a Blackfoot village, or he's gone under. Either way, there ain't shit we can do to help him."

Finch spat into the fire. "Let's give it one more day. Alex deserves that much."

"No," Sharp said flatly. "We got our women and all to worry about." When he saw Finch about ready to launch into an argument, he held his hand up. "No, Caleb. It's done for now. I'll miss Alex as much as ye will, but we cain't do nothin' for him now. I'll promise ye this, though: Soon's spring comes, I'll be headin' east again. We'll either take Alex back from them goddamn Blackfeet, or we'll raise hair enough to help his spirit get to the great beyond."

Finch grumbled, but he accepted it. He would hold Sharp to his promise; he'd be damned if he didn't.

23

The next day was a repeat of the last, though going in the opposite direction. They took turns holding the horses, pounding down snow and then hauling the animals up another few feet. The first five miles were relatively easy, since they had done all the work of flattening snow the day before, but once they passed the camp where they had waited out the storm, it grew bad again. The wind rose in the afternoon, and the temperature plummeted, making things worse. Their beards were coated with ice and their hands and feet were numb.

They finished off the jerky that night in a camp that was cheered only by the warmth of the fire. They had no coffee, and eating the jerky was like chewing frozen leather. Both men were tired and they ached all over.

A shot woke Finch in the morning, and he rolled

out of his robe, ignoring the cold. Rifle in hand, he crouched, silent, unmoving. Dawn was just breaking, and he could see a little way. A movement caught his eye, and he threw the gun up to his shoulder. Then he recognized Sharp.

Sharp strode up with a bloody package over his shoulder. "Meat," he said, as he dropped it on the ground near the fire. He sank down next to it, exhausted.

"Well, I'll be damned," Finch said, looking at the deer meat wrapped in hide. "I thought we was facin' starvin' times for sure."

"Me, too. Guess our medicine's gittin' better. I was in the bushes when I jumped that critter."

They built up the fire and gorged on the meat.

"Well, that was somethin' my meatbag took a shine to," Finch said as he leaned back, patting his stomach. He filled his pipe, noting that he had only enough tobacco for one more.

"Yep. And if we don't git too greedy, it ought to last us till we git back to camp."

They left soon after, but it was slow going. Occasionally they would find a patch of land where the wind had cleared the snow away, but these were few and far between and mighty small when they were found.

Finch and Sharp finally made it back. They had been gone more than two weeks and rode into camp hungry, weary, cold, and dispirited.

As soon as she saw them, Morning Sun began wailing in mourning. The two men ignored her as they dismounted. Many Bells took the animals away to care for them, while Finch and Sharp went into Finch's lodge. Dancing Feather served them food, and made sure the fire was burning well.

Annoyed, Finch finally said to Dancing Feather, "Git her to shet her trap, woman. Tell her we ain't sure Alex's dead."

"We think he's still alive," Sharp added helpfully.

Dancing Feather went outside and returned to the lodge moments later with a reasonably calm Morning Sun. They sat near the fire with the men, and Finch explained what had gone on. He ended with, "So ye see, we figure he's been took as a prisoner and that he's still alive."

"We aim to head out soon's the weather breaks," Sharp added. "We'll find him for ye."

It seemed to mollify the woman, at least enough to keep her quiet.

Finch fretted throughout the winter. Campbell's capture galled him to no end, and he blamed it all on himself. Had he listened to Sharp at the beginning and not split them up to run their traps, Campbell wouldn't have been taken. He was absolutely sure of that, even though Sharp tried to disabuse him of the idea.

So he worked and fretted and grumbled at the snow and cold and the frigid water and anything else he thought of. Winter would end, eventually, he knew, but with his desire for it to happen, it seemed to take forever.

The months passed, and one morning when Finch stepped out of his lodge, he sensed that spring was not far off. He wasn't sure what it was. The temperature was still well below freezing, and they had had more snow the night before, but he just sensed something different.

Winter returned with a vengeance the next morning,

dropping more than half a foot of new snow on the already blanketed ground. But Finch had sensed spring in the air, and he knew it would not be long now before he and the others could head off looking for Campbell.

Finch estimated it was about mid-April when he decided the time had come. "We'll leave out day after tomorrow," he told everyone.

"Little early, ain't it?" Sharp asked.

"Might be, but I cain't set here on my ass doin' nothin' no longer. I aim to go find Alex. Ye promised to do so, too, but if that ain't where your stick floats, ye take the women and head back toward the village. Or down to rendezvous. Me'n Alex'll find ye."

"Don't git your balls roarin', Caleb," Sharp said flatly. "I was jist askin'."

"Are ye comin' along, or ain't ye?" Finch demanded.

"'Course, I'm comin' along. Jesus."

"Glad that's settled."

"Ye plannin' to take the women and young'ns?" Sharp asked.

"Yep. I don't aim to come back this way, and I ain't gonna let 'em stay here by themselves in the spring, when the Blackfeet and every other goddamn Indian's gonna be ready to make war."

Sharp nodded. It was the argument he had planned to make if Finch had said he wasn't planning to take them along.

They hauled in their traps for the last time and moved out. It would be hard going, since the horses were still gaunted down from the winter. They moved slowly, picking their way carefully. Snow was still deep in many places and patches of ice made the going treacherous in spots.

They moved almost due east, through high, snow-filled passes, around peaks, across glades, spending long days on the trail. Hunting was good, though, so they ate well on elk, moose, and deer, and even occasionally buffalo. Grass was beginning to sprout, and that helped the animals considerably. They did not bother to trap, being more interested in getting to Blackfoot country and finding Campbell. They figured they could trap again later if they could find Campbell. Or learn that he was dead.

About a week out, they began seeing plenty of Blackfoot sign. "Must be gittin' near a village," Sharp said.

"I was thinkin' the same. We'd best hole up somewhere so me'n ye can take us a look-see."

"One of us best stay with the women and young'ns."

Finch nodded. They rode on, and soon found a spot they thought would be a suitable haven. When they got there, they decided that Finch, being the more rash of the two, would stay behind while Sharp would scout out the area. Sharp headed out just before dark. Finch had a sleepless night waiting for him. Sharp returned about an hour after dawn.

"Well?" Finch demanded impatiently.

Sharp ignored him. He walked to the fire and took a swig of the coffee that sat there and then began filling his mouth with hunks of roasted elk meat. "Good fire ye got here, Caleb," he said seriously. "Cain't see the smoke at all."

Finch had been reluctant to start a fire, but then finally decided to do so. He made the fire carefully, so that it would produce little smoke, and what there was would be filtered through the trees. "What'd ye find out?" he asked, not acknowledging the compliment.

Sharp had finished eating and sat back with another mug of coffee. "If Alex's in that village, I didn't see him. And there's a passel of Blackfeet out there. Even if he is in there we ain't gonna have much chance of gittin' him out. Not without goin' under ourselves."

"How many are there?"

"I counted twenty-six lodges."

"Damn." Finch sat thinking. Then he nodded and stood. "Well, I reckon we ought to at least see if he's there. He ain't, we can move on, and fast. He is, maybe we can think of somethin'."

"What ye got in mind?"

"Ye jist watch over the women and young'ns. I don't aim to be gone long."

Sharp shrugged, but cautioned, "Don't ye go doin' nothin' foolish now, hoss."

Finch ignored him as he went and saddled the Appaloosa. He rode out, rifle in one hand, rope to an empty pack horse in the other. He was back before noon. A young Blackfoot warrior was bound and gagged, lying over the back of the pack horse. Finch grinned broadly. "This here young buck might be able to tell us somethin'," he said.

He gave the Appaloosa to Dancing Feather, then not gently tugged the Blackfoot off the other horse. He shoved the Indian toward the fire and then down to the ground. Finch squatted by him. "Ye understand English, boy?" he asked.

The Blackfoot looked at him blankly.

Finch cut his hands loose and switched to using sign language. "There was a white man taken captive by your people. He was young, tall, had red hair. Is he here?"

The warrior sat staring straight ahead, silent.

"I'm only going to ask one more time," Finch signed. He was furious.

Still the Indian refused to say anything.

Finch spoke to Sharp, but made the signs to the Blackfoot: "Take his scalp."

The Indian's eyes flickered as Sharp rose and pulled his knife. He did not fear the pain or even death. But, like most Indians out this way, the Blackfeet revered their hair, believing it an extension of the soul. He became more agitated as Sharp moved closer. As Sharp's hand grabbed his hair, the Blackfoot's own hands suddenly flew in sign language: "The red-haired one isn't with us."

Sharp let go of the warrior's hair, and Finch asked, "Where is he?"

"He ran away. Two moons ago."

"Where'd he go?" Finch asked, surprised.

"I don't know. He went south. We followed for a while but couldn't find him."

"Damn," Finch said, looking up at Sharp. "He left out in the dead of winter. I misdoubt he made it, but he could have."

Sharp nodded. "Where ye think he was headed?"

"Hell if I know. There ain't a damn thing but Indians in any direction. Or maybe a camp of trappers. Finding one of them, though, would take a heap of traveling, and a heap of luck."

As they talked, the young Blackfoot jumped up and ran. Sharp grabbed his rifle, but Finch stopped him. Sharp nodded, realizing they could not allow a gunshot.

Finch ran and jumped on the Appaloosa and raced after the Blackfoot. As he roared past the running

Indian, he swiped at him with his tomahawk. The metal blade split the warrior's head, and he fell in a heap. Finch left him there, not even bothering to scalp him.

"What now, hoss?" Sharp asked as Finch came up and dismounted.

"I reckon the first thing is to get the hell away from here. Someone finds that buck and this place'll be swarmin' with fuckin' Blackfeet."

"Where to?"

Finch had to think about that for a while. Then he said, "We head back to Tall Clouds's village. Then we'll go with them to rendezvous. If Alex is alive and his medicine was strong, he might've found some trapper camp. If so, he'll be down there at rendezvous waitin' for us."

"And if he ain't?"

"Then we get a bunch of the Nay Percy and ride on back up here and start butcherin' Blackfeet," Finch said simply.

"That shines with this ol' hoss," Sharp said. His eyes were bright with anticipation.

Finch nodded. "I aim to make it fast, Ethan."

"Then let's ride."

Within half and hour, they were riding out of their camp. They moved west for several hours, then turned a little more south. Finch considered taking them almost straight south, figuring the plains were a lot easier to travel than the mountains. But that would leave them much too open to discovery by Blackfeet. So they headed up into the mountains before turning south. They moved fast, stopping only after it was dark. They were on the trail before dawn.

Only once did they come close to being detected.

They had been on the trail from the Blackfoot village almost a week when Sharp, bringing up the rear, stopped on a cliff and looked out over the country-side. He spotted a band of Blackfoot coming, and alerted Finch. They found a cave, large enough to hold all the people, as well as all the animals, and waited it out, tense.

The Blackfeet rode by two hundred yards away, not even noticing. The group decided to stay in the cave till the next morning, just in case the Blackfeet stopped nearby.

They were following the Swan River, continuing on through the valley between two looming mountain ranges, and eventually heading southwest, skirting some of the peaks.

"We gonna take Lolo Pass?" Sharp asked a few days later.

Finch shook his head. "Nope. We head south. A few days, a week maybe, we'll be on the Snake River Plain. We'll head southwest across that till we hit the Snake. If the Nay Percy're headin' for rendezvous, maybe we can cut their trail somewhere along in there. If not, we can head west then, heading straight for the valley where Tall Clouds usually winters."

Sharp nodded. It was as good a plan as any. Things had been so strange since Campbell had been taken captive that he expected everything and nothing.

24

They made a fine, though decidedly sad group when they rode into the Nez Percé village, despite the swirling escort of happy young warriors. The latter could not understand the gloom that clung to Finch, Sharp, Many Bells, Dancing Feather, Morning Sun and the children. The noise and smells and sights of the village were pleasing to the travelers; it seemed a long time since they had been there last. They only wished Campbell could be there to enjoy it all with them.

As they rode into the rough center of the camp, Campbell came bursting out from behind a lodge. He had been busy down by the stream when he had heard the commotion, and he just knew it was the arrival of his woman and his friends.

He ran full tilt toward them, shouting, "Caleb! Ethan! You're here!" But he ran right past the two astonished mountain men, stopping in a small cloud of dust beside Morning Sun's pony. Grinning from ear

214

BUCKSKINS AND BLOOD / 215

to ear, he reached up, grabbed her, ready to pull her down off the horse. Then he realized she was very, very pregnant. Almost shaking with joy, he helped her down, but gently. He was afraid to hug Morning Sun, lest he hurt her in her condition.

Morning Sun had no reticence, though. She grabbed him and pulled him close, holding him as if she would never let him go again.

"Lord, I missed ye, Morning Sun," Campbell breathed as he clung to her. "I dinna think I'd e'er see your sweet face again. And now here ye are. And with chil'." He couldn't help himself. He squeezed her hard and then released her as he did a little dance around her, whooping and hollering.

Morning Sun laughed at his antics, as the trappers and Nez Percé shouted ribald remarks, which Campbell pretended to ignore. Finally he stopped his celebrating, so he could hug Morning Sun again.

Campbell's impromptu demonstration of joy had given Finch and Sharp a few minutes to recover from the shock of seeing the Scotsman alive and well in the village. When Campbell stopped dancing, Finch said dryly, "Well lookee here, Ethan. We take that ol' chil' in and help him, keep the ol' coon alive, teach him everything he knows, go out searchin' for him when he gets took by the Blackfeet, and he ain't even got the goodness of heart to greet us two critters."

"It's enough to anger even an angel, let alone two sinful, crusty ol' beavers like us," Sharp agreed.

Campbell released Morning Sun, giving her a peck on the tip of her nose. Then he turned to face his two friends, who had dismounted. Solemnly he shook their hands. "I dunna quite know how to greet ye properly," he said seriously.

"Well I'll show ye, goddammit," Finch growled. He stepped forward and gave Campbell a bear hug that the Scotsman was sure was going to break his spine.

A moment later, Sharp had done the same.

"Well, we best pay our respects to Tall Clouds," Finch said to Campbell. "Then ye can tell us how ye come to be hyar."

Campbell nodded.

They met in Coyote Leggings's lodge, where Campbell had been staying since he had gotten back to the village, after Finch and Sharp had taken the time to pay their respects to Tall Clouds. When they arrived at the lodge, Stone Buffalo, Stands in the Water and Talks of War were waiting with Campbell.

At the small fire inside, as the women worked in the background, the men ate a little, then smoked, as Campbell recounted his story, including his confrontation, if that's what it could be called, with Beesley, Knebel, and Acosta. "Hell," he concluded, "I come back here with more plews than I would've had I ne'er been taken by the Blackfeet, what with gettin' the whole take from those three scoundrels."

"Ye sure had yourself an adventuresome winter, didn't ye, boy," Finch said when Campbell was finished.

"Aye."

"That shines, boy. Plumb shines." He paused, then asked seriously, "Ye doin' all right now?"

"Aye. I'm shinin' again." He paused. "Now, what about ye laddies? How'd ye spend your winter?"

Finch explained it, ending with, "Not so adventuresome as yours, mebbe, but we had us some times, though." Finch pulled his pipe out of his mouth and looked at the smoke curling up from the clay bowl for a moment. Then he looked at Campbell. "Now that you've had yourself some shinin' doin's over the winter, ye ready to head on down to the Siskidee and trade in our plews? Seems like we're due a proper spree."

"I'm nae ready to do that just yet, lads," Campbell said flatly. "I'm going after Talkin' Wolf. I'm not aboot to let that painted bastard get away wi' what he did to me. Nae. Besides, he's got my rifle, the one I won off Ol' Gabe. I promised mysel'—and Gabe—that I'd get it back. I was just waitin' to see if ye lads showed up."

Finch grinned. "Jist what I was wantin' to hear, boy," he said harshly. "I jist got me a hankerin' to head into Blackfoot country again. Jist to see the sights, mind ye."

"I were thinkin' the same thing," Sharp interjected.

"I canna ask ye to do that, lads," Campbell said. "I'll go mysel'—wi' a few of the Nay Percy who've said they wouldna mind the journey."

"Ye ain't keepin' this ol' coon out of such doin's," Finch said vehemently.

"Me neither," Sharp added.

Campbell grinned then. "Aye," he said with a nod. "I'll be happy to have ye along wi' me."

Finch looked at Stone Buffalo. "The *Nimipu* made meat for the spring yet?" he asked.

The Nez Percé nodded. "There's nothing to delay us leaving soon," he said.

"That suit ye, hoss?" Sharp asked Campbell.

"Aye. The sooner the better."

They fell silent then, thinking, planning, wondering what the future would bring. Then Sharp said, "It's a bit longer, but I reckon we ought to head along the Snake, heading generally toward rendezvous. That way the People'll be together and safe. Once we hit the plains, we can send them on toward the Siskidee, whilst we can ride hard north, straight up the plains along the mountains till we hit Talkin' Wolf's."

The others pondered that a bit, then one by one nodded, accepting the reasonableness of the plan.

They feasted and danced that night as the village welcomed the travelers back, until they finally collapsed, sated. All except Campbell and Morning Sun, who slipped off to their lodge early and had their own little celebration.

In the morning, Finch asked Campbell, "When're ye fixin' to leave, boy?"

"Tomorrow, if Tall Clouds is willin'."

"Let's go talk to him about it."

Tall Clouds, of course, knew about the plan and was just waiting for Campbell to come to him with it. After a long speech, during which he fell asleep twice for brief periods, he agreed that the Nez Percé would break camp in the morning and head east.

Two weeks later, the trappers and a band of warriors were ready to break away from the main band. The night before that was to happen, Campbell asked Finch, "Does Ol' Gabe know how to read?"

"Not a lick, boy. Why?"

"I owe him for the horse and supplies and such he let me have. I'd like to see if he can trade my plews in for me, take out what I owe him and hold the rest. I dunna expect we'll get back from Blackfoot country before rendezvous breaks up." He, like the others, gave no thought to the possibility of not coming back at all.

"Not a bad idea, boy," Finch said. "What do ye think, Ethan?"

Sharp nodded. "Shines with this chil'. Ol' Gabe'll

probably even arrange supplies for us for next season and give 'em over to the Nay Percy."

"Do it, boy," Finch said.

"But what good will it do, if he canna read?"

"Hell, somebody there'll read it to him."

"I trust Ol' Gabe, and I know ye two do, too, but do ye trust whoe'er it be he gets to read the letter to him?" Campbell asked.

"Yep," Finch said without hesitation. "Whoever reads it to him knows Ol' Gabe'll have his hair and his balls if he don't read it true."

That was good enough for Campbell. It took some time, but they finally found a sheet of paper and a pencil somewhere in one of Sharp's packs. With Finch and Sharp's help, Campbell carefully composed his letter and laboriously printed it out on the paper. When done, he folded it and encased it in a piece of leather. Then he gave it to Stands in the Water, who would be responsible for getting it to Bridger.

The war party left the next morning, heading north. They made quite a spectacle—twenty-three painted Nez Percé warriors and three buckskinned white men all mounted on painted, decked out ponies. They rode proudly, almost arrogantly, their backs straight, unafraid. All the warriors had guns, gotten in trade down at the rendezvous over the years, but they all also packed their well-known horn bows and quivers of arrows. In addition, most carried a lance, shield, knife, war club, and hatchet. There were no coup sticks among them. This was a raid for blood, not for counting coup. They wanted revenge for the mistreatment of one of their own—Campbell—not honors.

They traveled light and fast. Since there were no women or children along, they were unencumbered.

They had no pack animals, either. They would hunt along the way, and each man carried a small coffeepot and supply of coffee beans. As they rode, hunters fanned out, bringing down buffalo, elk, deer, and antelope. They ate well, and believed that showed how strong their medicine was.

They became more wary as they began edging into Blackfoot country. The Nez Percé were brave men, and held no fear of anyone, but they were not fools. The Blackfeet were a mighty nation, warlike and vicious, but as courageous and as fierce as any. The Nez Percé were not afraid, but they were not taking their enemy lightly. Scouts were placed far out front and behind, and to each flank. They would not be surprised.

As they neared the land where Talking Wolf's village had been, the warriors began making offerings to the spirits, increasing their medicine so they would be better prepared for battle.

One night, when they were only a day or so away from the Milk River, Finch asked Campbell, "Ye aim to take on the whole fuckin' Blackfoot Nation, boy? Or are ye jist out for Talking Wolf?"

"I hadna thought of it much. I suppose I'd be satisfied with just Talking Wolf—and the five others he had wi' him when they took me—but we might have to take them all on to do it. It depends on them, I suppose."

Campbell had entertained thoughts that he and his two trapper friends might be able to slip into Talking Wolf's camp and just grab him. Those thoughts fled the next morning, though, when a Blackfoot hunting party spotted them. The hunting party raced off after a brief clash, leaving one of their men dead.

"Looks like the decision's been made now, boy,"

Finch said to Campbell. "We got us a fight on our hands sure as shit now."

Half an hour later, a large band of Blackfeet showed up on the horizon, riding hard toward them. The Nez Percé scouts were called back in, and the Nez Percé stopped, spreading out in a long line. The Blackfeet did the same about fifty yards away.

A brawny Blackfoot rode out in front of his men a little and began haranguing the Nez Percé in his own language.

"That's Talking Wolf," Campbell snarled. He went to kick his horse into motion, but the strong arms of Finch on one side and Coyote Leggings on the other stopped him.

"Jist set, boy," Finch said quietly.

Campbell looked at his partner, his face a mask of fury. "Ye canna tell me what to do, Caleb Finch," he snarled. "I'm going to get that bastard, and I'm nae aboot to let anyone—even ye—stop me."

"Don't git your dander up, boy," Finch said calmly. "You'll git him. I already started passin' word to everybody that Talkin' Wolf's yours. But you'll wait till Talks of War gives the word afore ye go after him."

Talks of War had gone out in front of the Nez Percé and was insulting the Blackfeet, much as Talking Wolf was doing to the Nez Percé, though neither could understand the other.

Campbell watched him a few moments, trying to relax. "Why're they insultin' each other?" he finally asked.

"Ye undersand Blackfoot, boy?" Finch asked, only a little surprised.

"Aye. Speak it, too."

Finch shook his head. "Well, boy, you're about

the only one here can understand both sides. The Blackfeet can't understand the Nay Percy and the other way around. But that don't mean much, though. They know the other's not offerin' pleasantries. It's as much to build up their own men as much it is to insult the other side."

Campbell nodded and sat, fidgeting. "We e'er gonna get to fightin'?" Campbell finally grumbled. "All they're doon is sittin' there callin' each other names."

"Sooner or later," Finch said. He was almost as eager as Campbell for things to commence, but one couldn't tell it by looking at him.

The challenging and haranguing dragged on and on, and Campbell grew more and more impatient. "How long's this shit going to go on?" he asked, voice harsh.

"Hours mebbe."

"I canna stand it nae more," Campbell muttered. Before Finch or Coyote Leggings could stop him, Campbell snapped his musket up to his shoulder and fired off a shot.

As the echo of the gunfire drifted away in the strong plains wind, silence descended. Then, raising his arm, Talking Wolf screeched a war cry and fired his rifle. Both sides charged at the same time.

25

Campbell tried keeping his eyes on Talking Wolf, but the Blackfoot war leader let his warriors rush by as he reloaded his rifle. Campbell reloaded on the run. Then Campbell was in the midst of a whirling, mad battle, and he lost sight of Talking Wolf. In fact, it was hard to see anything.

Dust rose in billowing clouds, and horses bumped into one another as warriors hacked, slashed, and shot at one another. Some men from both sides jumped to the ground to fight on foot. A frightening din arose as men roared and horses screamed and whinnied wildly.

Through the haze, Campbell saw a Blackfoot aiming an arrow at Hawk Strikes. He rode up and shot the Indian in the back from close range, smashing the Blackfoot forward onto his face, dead. He kicked his horse, bucking and plunging through the swirling bedlam, until he was clear of it.

Campbell looked frantically around for Talking Wolf, worried that someone else would have killed him. Though all knew that Talking Wolf was Campbell's prey, in the heat of battle it might not be possible to leave the Blackfoot war leader for Campbell. Then he spotted him far off to the Blackfoot left flank, at the fringes of the battle. He disappeared and reappeared, apparently darting into battle to strike at a Nez Percé and then move to safety again to see where else he was needed.

Intent on the warrior he wanted to slay, Campbell never saw the Blackfoot who came charging out of the cloudiness. The Indian's horse smashed into Campbell's, and the Scotsman felt himself flying. He hit the ground and rolled, bouncing, grunting with the jolts. When he came to a stop, he had lost his musket, but he still had his pistol, tomahawk, and knife.

As he got up, Campbell saw the Blackfoot stalking toward him. The warrior was a big man, with broad shoulders, strong-looking arms and thick, powerful legs. His face was streaked with wide, jagged lines of red and yellow, and much of his chest was covered by a hair-pipe breastplate.

Campbell took a quick glance around and saw Talking Wolf even farther away from him now. He turned back to the warrior, who was only ten feet away and carried a bloody tomahawk in one huge hand. "Try this shit, laddie," Campbell said as he pulled his pistol from his belt and fired.

The ball ripped through the warrior's breastplate, and he staggered back a few steps before falling. He got up almost instantly, though, much to Campbell's surprise and annoyance. He came on again.

Campbell shoved his pistol away and pulled his

own tomahawk. He advanced on the Blackfoot, not wanting to give the massive warrior any advantage. He hacked the man down, much as he had Talking Wolf's son, Black Horse. It was over in moments, what with the Blackfoot almost unable to defend himself because of the pistol ball he carried in his chest.

Spotting a stray horse, Campbell leaped on it and raced off after Talking Wolf. But the two war parties had broken off now and were regrouping, Campbell saw as the dust settled a little. He suddenly felt vulnerable, trapped behind enemy lines as he was.

The Blackfeet paid no attention to him, though, apparently not even knowing he was there. They charged again, and the Nez Percé fell back some under the assault. Talking Wolf was lost in the confusion again, and Campbell rode aimlessly, looking for the Blackfoot leader.

He saw Finch and then Sharp and Coyote Leggings. The three seemed to be everywhere, darting in to strike down an enemy and then move on to help another Nez Percé. Furious, Campbell moved around the fringes of the chaos, looking, always looking.

Then the forces split again and pulled back, bringing their dead and wounded with them. Campbell's eyes narrowed as he saw Talking Wolf exhorting his warriors. Not caring a bit that he was all alone in the face of two dozen or more Blackfeet, Campbell charged, determined to get Talking Wolf.

Both sides had charged again, though, and he was swept up in the depths of the milling, screeching warriors. The battle closed around him, almost deafening him with its pandemonium. "Damn!" he screamed in frustration as he whacked at a Blackfoot who had tried to club him in the head. He missed, but as he tried to turn for another slash at the warrior, the Blackfoot went down, a Nez Percé lance in his side. Hawk Strikes grinned a little at Campbell as he jerked his lance from the Blackfoot's body.

Then Hawk Strikes was gone, and Campbell spotted Talking Wolf, moving like a phantom in and out of the battle. Campbell urged his panicky, stolen horse through the mass of men and animals, hacking and slashing his way along. When he got into the clear, he saw Talking Wolf off to one side, alone, switching his tired mount for a fresher one.

Campbell started in that direction, but something caught the corner of his eye. He glanced to his right and saw that Talks of War had fallen after being knocked from his horse. The older warrior had gotten up and stood haughtily, unafraid of his enemies, singing his death song.

Campbell hesitated. His enemy, the man he had sworn to kill, was there before him, alone, vulnerable. Then he shook his head. He could not leave his father-in-law, one of the most revered war leaders of the Nez Percé, who was facing two Blackfeet now, with two others moving up rapidly. The latter would reach Talks of War before his friends would.

Whirling his horse, he raced toward Talks of War. From beyond the Nez Percé, he could see Finch and Hawk Strikes galloping toward Talks of War, too. Sharp was also coming, but was much farther off. Then a horse tore past Campbell, a screaming demon on its back. It was Coyote Leggings, out to save his uncle, the man who had taught him to be a warrior, a man, a *Nimipu*.

Coyote Leggings flew off his horse and hit one of

the Blackfeet. Moments later, Campbell, Finch, and Hawk Strikes arrived at about the same time and formed a protective circle around Talks of War. Coyote Leggings was horrifying in his violence. After hitting the one Blackfoot, his knife flashed once, and the Blackfoot was laid open from crotch to breastbone. Then he spun and wrenched the other enemy from Talks of War's grasp. The knife moved again in a blur, and the Blackfoot's neck suddenly was spurting blood.

Finch and Hawk Strikes had made quick work of the other two Blackfeet, but two more had broken through the circle, trying to save their comrades. Campbell jumped off his pony onto those two Blackfeet, and all three men fell to the ground. Campbell kicked one and punched the other as they tried to gain their feet. Then he leaped onto one, waiting for a tomahawk in the back.

That never came, but he did feel the cold steel of a knife slice his back, though it did not seem to be very deep. He ignored that, hoping that someone else would get the Blackfoot who had slashed him, while he concentrated on the one he had in his grasp.

He smashed the Indian's face with his forehead and then choked the warrior, sitting on him. In moments, the Blackfoot was dead. Campbell jumped up and spun. Since he had not been attacked again, he figured someone had taken care of the other Blackfoot. He saw Coyote Leggings peeling the warrior's scalp.

Blackfeet were pouring toward them now, though, apparently realizing that they had the Nez Percé war leader, as well as all the white men in one spot, since Sharp had arrived. But the Blackfeet underestimated the ferocity of the tight little band. Finch and Sharp, now the only ones mounted, rode back and forth in insane fury, struggling, swearing, chopping, and howling.

The ones on the ground were no less savage. The Blackfeet began to fall back, awed by the rage of their enemies. Talks of War was wounded in the heat of it all, though slightly, as was Coyote Leggings.

More Nez Percé began arriving, and the Blackfeet broke and ran, taking their dead and wounded with them when they could, though a few were left behind. Campbell saw his chance. He looked around for a horse. Then Finch was at his side. "Hyar, boy, take mine." He held out the reins to the Appaloosa. "Jist take good care of him, boy," Finch added as Campbell leaped into the saddle.

Campbell kicked the horse, enjoying the feeling of strength and power in the animal under him. He raced off, searching for Talking Wolf. He finally spotted the Blackfoot, leading his warriors away. Campbell did not slow down. He was unafraid of the Blackfeet. Some of the Nez Percé had followed him, and would help protect him, but that mattered only a little. Campbell had his bloodlust up. He would ride through hell to get this Indian.

Campbell began passing Blackfeet, but none bothered him. They were too dispirited. Campbell never took his eyes off Talking Wolf's back. The Blackfoot leader finally looked back and saw Campbell. He kicked his horse into a run. But the pinto was no match for the big Appaloosa, and Campbell easily closed the gap. Campbell rode alongside Talking Wolf, who swiped ineffectually at him with his own rifle. Campbell pulled a little ahead and then bumped Talking Wolf's pinto slightly. He did it twice more, and on the fourth contact, the pinto began to turn.

Once more and the Blackfoot was riding back the way he had come.

As they began passing more Blackfeet going the other way, Campbell grabbed his empty pistol and walloped Talking Wolf across the side of the head with it.

Talking Wolf grunted and almost lost his seat on the horse, but he managed to hang on.

Campbell clubbed him over the ear again, and Talking Wolf fell sideways, pulling the pinto with him. The horse squealed and fell, but it scrambled up and ran off. Campbell pulled to a stop and turned the Appaloosa, watching as Talking Wolf stood, now surrounded by Nez Percé.

Campbell dismounted and picked up the rifle he had won from Bridger. He looked it over carefully. It seemed to be in fine shape, though dirty from having been fired a couple of times. He walked over to stand in front of Talking Wolf. "Run," he said in Blackfoot. Then in English, he said, "Go on and run, ye son of a bitch."

Talking Wolf stood, looking blank, seemingly unfazed by Campbell's words or his own bleeding head.

"I'm gonna give ye more of a chance than ye gave me, Talking Wolf," Campbell said tightly. "Now run." He shoved Talking Wolf's shoulder, half turning him. He did so again, spinning him to face away from him. "Run!" he roared, kicking Talking Wolf in the buttocks.

The Blackfoot began to run, trotting at first, but building up his speed. When Talking Wolf was about a hundred yards away, Campbell took off running, rifle in hand. The Nez Percé and two other trappers followed, most of them on horseback, yelling encouragement.

Campbell caught up and jammed his rifle between Talking Wolf's legs. The Blackfoot went tumbling head first. He got back up and began running again, limping a little as the Nez Percé laughed and hooted at him.

Then Talking Wolf stopped and turned to face Campbell. "You're no match for a Blackfoot, Worm," he said. "I will run no more. If you think you can kill me, do it."

Campbell was incensed at being called "Worm." He set down his rifle and pulled his knife. Talking Wolf also drew his blade. The Nez Percé grew quiet as they watched the two men facing each other.

As Campbell drew closer to Talking Wolf, the Blackfoot knelt swiftly, scooped up a handful of dirt and threw it in Campbell's face. Campbell staggered back a step or two, dropping his knife and trying to clear his vision with both hands.

Talking Wolf jumped at Campbell, who managed to grab the Blackfoot's knife arm. The two men stood, struggling, sweating, grunting. Then they fell and rolled, each fighting to end on top, gaining the advantage. Campbell's left hand slipped off Talking Wolf's shirt, but in so doing, the elbow smacked Talking Wolf's nose. It was just enough to loosen Talking Wolf's grip on Campbell.

Campbell spun away, looking for his knife. He saw it and snatched it up, just about the time Talking Wolf slammed into him. They rolled apart, and jumped up. Campbell had lost his knife again, but Talking Wolf had managed to come up with his. Raising the weapon high, Talking Wolf charged.

Campbell's left hand stopped the descending knife. With his right hand, he pounded Talking Wolf in the stomach and chest, his hard, callused fist battering the Blackfoot. The warrior sagged, and Campbell let go of his knife arm. Then he pulled his tomahawk. Holding the weapon in both hands, Campbell swung it for all he was worth at the teetering Talking Wolf. The blade just about severed Talking Wolf's head, and the Blackfoot fell, body dancing in an odd jerking motion on the ground.

Campbell stood, bent at the waist, hands on knees, breathing heavily. Sweat dripped from the tip of his nose.

A knife suddenly appeared quivering in the dirt next to him. As he stared stupidly at it, he heard Finch say, "Well, now, boy, raise his hair and let's go on home."

Campbell looked up and saw Finch grinning at him. "Ye heard me, boy," he said lightly. "Our business is done here, and ye got yourself a carin' wife back yonder. And, by Christ, probably a chil' by now, too. This ain't no time for stallin'."

"Aye," Campbell said, smiling and straightening. "Aye."

JOHN LEGG is a full-time writer and newspaper editor who lives in Arizona with his family.